Redstripe

and Other Dachshund Tales

Redstripe

and Other Dachshund Tales

By Jack Magestro

Redstripe
Bernard
Bernard's Visit
The Mouse That Was Saved
The Real Christmas Story

Unlimited Publishing
Bloomington, Indiana

First Edition

Copies of this book and others
are available to order online at:

http://www.unlimitedpublishing.com/authors

ISBN 1-58832-078-2

Unlimited Publishing
Bloomington, Indiana

Contents

Prologue to "Redstripe"

MANY OF THE PEOPLE we have met during our many travels may remember us; Jack and Jill and Belle. Our names really *are* Jack and Jill so most folks don't have a tough time remembering us. We introduce ourselves as "Jack and Jill—really". Jill and I met a while back after we had both experienced our own failures with the institution of marriage. Belle is our dachshund. She is a ten pound smooth miniature female. She is a little lamb with an attitude usually held in check.

Long ago (at least in the realm of cyberspace it seems long ago) we started to write back and forth over the internet with others we met during our travels to Mexico and the Caribbean. In this day and age, everyone has an e-mail address and shares it. Lots of information was exchanged between our discovered friends and us over time over the net. Many stories were traded and many life experiences, good and bad, unfolded on our computer monitor. We learned of career changes, planned trips and met friends. We were updated about families and woes and concerns. We were informed of the births of babies and grandbabies, and read about dark hours and joyful days.

We shared our own trials and tribulations with these friends. Often, over the internet, we shared the adventures and misadventures of our own travels.

This group of friends, whose homes are located from Canada to Australia, has remained in touch with each other over a very long period. We have never met face-to-face all at one time. But our contacts have remained in place due to the efforts of some very special people.

For some reason or another, there seems to have grown an incredible bond between all of us. Joined through the internet only because we had met while vacationing in one Caribbean spot or another, we have come to rely upon each other via e-mail during grim days and have rejoiced with one another the same way during sunny times.

It is for this group that the "Redstripe" story was put into actual words. It is for them; our friends.

We must thank Carol and Sue, two members of the group who helped organize things for us for this story and made sure we had all of the little parts together.

And we must thank Sam. He has continued to orchestrate our group connections over the net. Look for him in Texas. He is a gray haired guy who sometimes rides a big motorcycle. Should you want to find him, just approach every biker in Texas who has gray hair and ask if the guy has dachshunds. If he squints at you and appears annoyed, run. When one says yes, you will have found Sam.

This is a story about Jamaica that involves a dachshund. Or it may be a story about a dachshund that involves Jamaica. It's hard to say. You decide. In any event, this is a treasured family story that has taken some time to discover during our many trips from the United States to Jamaica and back. You are free to believe the story or not. We make no claim that the story is fact. The first section is about to begin, and please be warned—you may have trouble concentrating on other important matters until you read the end. So, get a glass of rum, grab this little tale and put your feet up.

REDSTRIPE

A Tale of a New York Dachshund

ON ONE OF OUR TRIPS to Jamaica, we ran into a rastamafarian named Cirtron. Now, if you don't know what a rastamafarian is, well, it is easy to explain. Sort of. Rastamafarians believe in "GA." GA is god. And one of the main beliefs of the rastamafarians is that it is just fine to consume an awful lot of "ganja." Ganga is marijuana. "GA" is said to acknowledge this consumption and it seems to be accepted in Jamaica that the "rasta" men smoke a great deal of marijuana. Our Cirtron is no exception.

Cirtron is black. He is night-black. He has a short wiry frame usually covered only by a pair of khaki pants—no shirt. One does not see him much in the light of day and he is usually stoned at night. He makes his living weaving baskets and bracelets that he sells to the tourists he finds as he wanders the beaches of Negril. His black hair cascades down and around his shoulders in dreadlocks.

He also functions as an "escort" to a certain class of lonely or adventurous gals looking for something new. And yes that escort service is exactly what it implies. In fact, the literature from the Jamaican tourism board warns about people like Cirtron. But Cirtron is a happy and carefree man, would not harm a flea (or the dachshund on which it lived) and we have found him to be reasonably trustworthy and a good friend. Of course, he is not someone who understands a clock.

When we first met Cirtron, he told us of a trip he took to New York to visit a "girlfriend" he had met (escorted) while the lady was visiting Jamaica. It is Cirtron's trip to New York that marks the beginning of the story,

It seems that a young woman named Sheila had taken a liking to Cirtron during her vacation to the island. She was so taken with him that she wrote him when she returned home and eventually paid for a plane ticket so that Cirtron could travel to see her in New York. Sheila was a bit wild and she knew what she wanted. She wanted Cirtron, dreadlocks and all; in part to show him off to her friends.

Sheila worked in an insurance agency assembling various quotes and documents for the people responsible to underwrite various contracts. She lived in a six-story brownstone apartment building with no elevator. Her apartment was on the fourth floor and she had two bedrooms with windows that faced the street. The apartment had a small bath, walk-in kitchen and a living room with cheap prints of the work of Georgia O'Keefe in expensive frames on the walls. Sheila was gorgeous. She was blonde, slim, had hair that cascaded down her back like a waterfall and was prone to wearing tight clothing and stiletto heels. She could turn a lot of heads.

When Sheila picked Cirtron up at the airport and then drove him to her home, he was amazed. Cirtron's home was in the hills of Jamaica with his family and the various aunts, uncles, lots of pigs, goats, chickens and children. A visitor would have no exact idea of who the parents of the children are; it doesn't matter. They are all loved in Cirtron's extended family. Cirtron was not prepared for the trip and the plane. But he knew what a house was and he was stunned by Sheila's apartment. Running water? HOT water?! Oh, mon!

Sheila had a dachshund. A female dachshund that had just delivered three puppers eight weeks before Cirtron arrived.

New York and Cirtron

Cirtron spent a month and a bit more in New York with Sheila. He became a great friend and buddy of Paris, Sheila's mom dachshund. Sheila astounded Cirtron by taking him to all the right places in New York and making the rounds of the parties so many of her friends threw because, well, that's what they did. Cirtron was just as great a hit with Sheila's friends as he was with Paris. Paris was a bit of a greater hit with Cirtron than Sheila's friends.

Cirtron astounded Sheila with his ability to deal with cab drivers. He was good at this because back home, in Jamaica, his uncle drove a rundown old heap as a cab to help with the finances of Cirtron's extended family up in the hills. Cirtron had learned well from his uncle and the rules for cabbies in New York are no different than in Jamaica.

Rule one: get a fare. Rule two: keep him. Rule three: get a tip. Cirtron could deal with cab drivers and shamelessly negotiated the fare regardless of what the meter read. He explained to us how he had saved so many nickels and quarters left over from change after he had tipped the drivers. In spite of Cirtron's knack with cabs, we never have known if he really understood American money. A Jamaican dollar is only about one thirtieth of a U.S. dollar and yet he was adept (too much so) at trading "j's" for U.S. Changing from U.S. to U.S. was another matter for him, but somehow the cab driver always ended up short. Cirtron's uncle would have been proud. You'll learn more about him later.

Because Cirtron had taken such a liking to Paris and her puppies and because Sheila had such a soft spot and affinity for Cirtron, Sheila gave him one of the pups.

Now before we explain how the pup left the country with Cirtron, breaking through all kinds of rules and red tape, we need to explain the puppy's name. In Jamaica, the most predominant local beer is called "Red Stripe." It bears a red stripe on white on the label. It is rather a heavy beer. As an import in the United States it is expensive but in Jamaica it is cheap, common and plentiful. It's sort of like the local equivalent of an Old Style or an Old Milwaukee beer.

Cirtron and Sheila, in fond memory of their time in Jamaica, agreed the puppy's name would be Redstripe. Then they began to plan how to get the little dog out of the country and back to Jamaica with Cirtron.

The Airport

As part of their plan to get Redstripe to Jamaica with Cirtron while avoiding all kinds of red tape and quarantines, Sheila bought a ventilated gym bag for Cirtron to use as carryon luggage for his trip back to the island. You see, Redstripe is a mini-red dachshund. When she finally "grew up" she did not even tip the scales at eight pounds. As a little twelve-week-old puppy, she was not much more than two handfuls. She was probably only one handful for Cirtron. He had big hands. It's a Jamaican thing, we think. The ventilated gym bag had a specific purpose in the plan.

Sheila, of course, being Sheila, purchased a good amount of clothing for Cirtron during his visit. She always had her own view of how things should be. She equipped him with new jeans, an embroidered sweatshirt and docksiders; all for the trip home. She tried convincing him to take some silk boxers as well. They were not well received. Certain barriers exist between cultures. When Cirtron explained his reluctance to take the silk boxers, we understood. Somehow, skinny, black Cirtron, in paisley print silk boxers, wandering the beaches of the Caribbean, did not seem to fit our image of the rastamafarian.

You need to picture this, please, as Cirtron walks through the airport clutching boarding pass and plane ticket in an envelope from the airline.

Cirtron is ready to go. He is dressed in the sweatshirt with some catchy New York phrase embroidered on the front. He has new jeans. They are stiff. He has no jacket because he will not need it and his feet are without socks, encased only in the new smooth docksiders that fall and flip up against his heels as he walks. This American tourist look is in complete contrast to Cirtron the person and his color and hair and beard. Rastamafarians do not cut their hair, or beard, for that matter. And their locks tangle in long cascades of twisted dreadlocks. Part of this is due to their African ancestry. Part is due to the length of hair that is not combed out over years of time. The dreadlocks look like little tight fuzzy braids. Cirtron's reach to the middle of his back. It is almost a human mane.

Only his beard diminishes the dreadlocks. It is formidable, to say the least. We have joked that small children could hide in its largess.

The plan, of course, as you may have guessed, was to hide Redstripe in the ventilated gym bag taken as a carry on. So the little pupper was sedated and placed in the bag with the rest of Cirtron's things for the trip. We do not mean to imply that this is the way to treat dachshunds, but that is what we were told happened. We don't know what the sedative was and didn't ask.

Sheila accompanied Cirtron through the airport. Redstripe was in the bag, blissfully unaware, asleep and tunneled amongst Cirtron's clothes in the gym bag. Cirtron craned his neck about, trying to take in all of the sights of the busy airport. They had a major hurdle to deal with. They reached the mezzanine and it was time to check Cirtron's carry on through the x-ray machine and metal detector before proceeding to the gate for the plane.

Cirtron placed the bag; Redstripe snuggled inside, on the conveyor belt. Sheila watched with baited breath. Cirtron stepped through the portal of the metal detector and the bag moved forward through the hanging straps and disappeared into the depths of the machine.

The security man did not even blink an eye at Cirtron. There was a flight leaving soon for Jamaica, after all, and he was used to seeing the rasta men. Cirtron was not even wearing one of the red, green, black and yellow knit hats so common in Jamaica. Cirtron was invisible to the security man.

The belt brought the bag out the far end of the machine.

No one had noticed the skeleton shadow of the little dog on the screen. They were all too bored to pay attention. Cirtron snatched the bag and turned back to wave at Sheila. She smiled and waved back with a teary smile.

Cirtron and Redstripe were headed home. Next stop: Montego Bay.

Flying Dachshund

Most of Cirtron's and Redstripe's air trip back to Jamaica was uneventful. Cirtron had his lunch balanced precariously on the little fold down tray and managed to keep most of the food out of his beard. Redstripe slept on.

The East Coast of the United States drifted by beneath the right side of the airplane. Nothing but ocean showed to the left. Soon, the airplane headed off from the Florida coast and continued on over the waters around Cuba. Cuba looked green and peaceful from thirty thousand feet. The view belied the political strife that was so much a part of the history of the green and brown island.

Somewhere, just past the waters around Cuba, Redstripe began to wake.

At first Cirtron heard only a murmur from beneath his seat. Then he heard a snort and then a squeak. The bag began to jostle around and Cirtron became alarmed. "Ah, mon," he thought to himself, "dis be naht good." But before he could collect his thoughts and decide what to do, his seat partner, Andrea Sue, suddenly perked up and looked down over Cirtron's knee at the bag beneath his seat.

She said, "Mister? What's in your bag? It's *moving!*"

Andrea Sue was nine years old and her parents dozed in the two seats behind Cirtron. For many adults, Cirtron's appearance would have put them off. But children are not infected by the foibles of adults and Andrea Sue did not care who or what Cirtron was. She was interested only in that jostling gym bag. "Mister, what's in there?" she begged.

Cirtron said to Andrea Sue, "No problem, mon. Eezz jus mah dog. Be still little miss. Irie?"

"Can I see? Please, can I see?"

"Ahhh," said Cirtron. "I dunno. De dog, she be sleepy. Keen?"

Andrea Sue looked back to where her parents were sleeping in the next back seats and turned back to Cirtron. She was not about to be dismissed. She was nine.

"Please? Can I please see your dog, Mister?"

"Ahhh, little miss. Oh, kay. Irie. But not to tell, Ah?"

Cirtron leaned over and reached down to pull the bag from under his seat. He unzipped the lengthwise zipper. Andrea Sue peered into the bag and she saw two bright little black eyes gazing up. Those little eyes were a bit dazed, but ready to go and happy to see the little girl.

"Shsss, little miss," said Cirtron. "Not to tell. She be Redstripe and needs her sleep. Oh kay, mon?"

"Okay, man. I won't tell." Andrea Sue grinned hugely and scratched the little Redstripe on the top of the head. She allowed Cirtron to zip the bag and place it back under his seat and she settled back, aglow with her secret.

Montego Bay was just ahead. Andrea Sue's parents began to stir, as did the rest of the passengers, as the island of Jamaica came into view.

The plane, with Cirtron and Redstripe and Andrea Sue and her parents and the rest of the passengers, came down out of the sky toward the airstrip at Montego Bay. All could see the emerald ocean glisten in the Caribbean sun. Cirtron felt the pulse of the engines change and Redstripe started, alarmed, at the sound of the wheels chucking down for the landing. The plane bumped down and the roar of the engines, as the baffles came to play to reverse them, was nearly more felt than heard.

Andrea Sue leaned over to speak to Cirtron. "Where do you live? Is Redstripe going there too? Do you have other dogs for her to play with? Do you have children? Isn't it too hot here for little dachshunds? My mom told me it's hot here."

"Ahhh, chile. Ya' mon. All of dese tings. Redstripe, she be ta go wid me to de mountains. But, no. Naht to be too hot. Ga takes, he takes de care to look at all tings under de sun. Redstripe, she be happy, mon. And welcome to Jamaica, girl. Wanna say de good bye to da Redstripe?"

Andrea Sue certainly was not going to pass up that offer. So Cirtron unzipped the bag once again and Andrea Sue reached in to pet the little dog. She grinned back at Cirtron and then frowned. "She must be hungry!"

"Ya' mon! But de ladies, make her de goat 'soon as we get dere. She be eating well and me too. No problem, mon."

Cirtron rezipped Redstripe's temporary home as the passengers on the plane all got up to stretch and gather their bags from under the seats and from the overhead compartments. Andrea Sue's father gathered up his daughter with a jaundiced look at Cirtron.

Cirtron shrugged and said "Welcome to Jamaica, mon!"

Cirtron and Redstripe faced one more barrier. They had to pass the security at the Mo-Bay airport. Cirtron was hopeful, however. The security guards were more concerned with what left the country than with what came in.

Cirtron felt hopeful. He just needed for Redstripe to be still.

Security Check—Jamaican Style

After the plane landed and everyone had gotten up to gather their belongings and then stood in the aisle of the airplane to await their chance to depart, Cirtron joined the queue, Redstripe in the bag over his shoulder, to leave the plane too. There is no "tunnel" at the Mo-Bay airport leading from the plane to the terminal. An old fashioned set of steps is rolled up to the plane and everyone just clambers down right onto the tarmac. Cirtron stepped out of the plane and onto the first step as the heat hit like a warm moist mist.

It was quite a trek from the plane to the terminal and customs. Redstripe began to fidget.

She fidgeted a lot. Cirtron tried to calm the little creature without drawing attention. He opened the bag just enough to reach in and give Redstripe some air. "Ahhh, little dog, be still, mon, 'need to be quiet, keen?" And he rubbed Redstripe's neck and head.

Across the tarmac they trudged, down the corridors of the terminal, and then on to the security check. There were four lines with impatient and sweating Jamaican officials whom checked visas and passports and stamped this and that. Cirtron got his passport stamped, handed in the forms he had filled out on the plane about what and why and who he was, and then submitted his bag to the checkers. Sometimes these people opened things and sometimes they did not. It all depended on luck.

Luck was not in store for Cirtron and Redstripe this day.

Redstripe was just too excited and restless after being confined for so long in the gym bag to stay still. She wriggled and squirmed as the bag lay on the counter. And the checker saw the bag move.

"Ai! What you be carrying? Open it please, mon. What have you inside there?"

Now please, you need to understand about the Jamaican people. After all else, respect is most important. Trouble is just not part of the Jamaican view of the world and no one wants to offend. The checker was embarrassed to have to confront a fellow countryman. One people, one blood, means a lot. But duty called. And Cirtron would have to answer. He did. He answered in a silly and simple style that would simply not work in the United States. But in Jamaica, there is "no problem, mon!"

"Ya, mon, no problem, mon," said Cirtron and he slid the zipper open to the show the head of Redstripe. Her eyes shown out from the dim recesses of the bag expectantly, all but her head covered by Cirtron's clothes.

The checker was surprised, to say the least. "Wat is dese, mon? Ya may not move de dog to de country widout de quarantine and papers, mon. Ai!"

Please withhold your disbelief and judgment. Remember that this is in Jamaica.

Cirtron leaned over the counter and whispered in a conciliatory fashion. "No dog, mon. My sister's chile, mon. She de comeback wid me to home, mon."

What the checker said was not translatable. He issued a long stream of patois that no one not born on the island could understand.

Cirtron admonished the checker, "Dese is a chile of god, mon. I tell you, eez my sister's chile. Ya know, mon, sometime, de ladies smoke de ganga up in de hill, mon. Dese affect de chiles. Not always well. But she still be a chile of god, mon. My sister, she be de wait for her chile, mon."

Cirtron flashed his smile, yellow teeth in a black face, the most Sunday best he could muster.

The checker looked Cirtron in the eye and said, 'Hey, mon, what d'you tink, keeping de baby in de bag likkel dat? Have you no respect, mon?'

Cirtron just smiled as best he could.

Cirtron and Redstripe were passed through. And Redstripe was now officially, sort of anyway, in Jamaica. They went out the front of the terminal to look for Cirtron's uncle in the lane with all of the cabs and vans that took tourists to the resorts.

The checker remained and shook his head of black curls in amusement. He went on to check out the real problems—the American and European tourists.

Into the Mountains with Goats and Girls

Uncle Basi was there, out side of the Mo-Bay terminal. He had driven his 1969 Chevrolet Impala down from the cockpit country. This was Cirtron's transportation home. There were a few extra passengers on the trip, all installed on the broken and sun-split back seats, and one or two on the hood. As the tourists crowded into the busses and vans that would take them to the resorts and villas and other vacation destinations, a small plane took off from the main runway. It had as passengers those that had a few extra dollars to spend in order to avoid the road trip to the resorts in Ochos Rios, Runaway Bay and Negril. Basi hugged his nephew, and the nieces and others from the car piled out with their hellos on their lips for Cirtron.

Redstripe was still confined to the gym bag slung over Cirtron's shoulder.

Uncle Basi squandered quite a bit of money buying Ting and beers from the hawkers who all reached through the fence at the edge of the parking lot to sell to those just arriving. The hawkers were not allowed on the airport grounds, but did a brisk business through the fence. Basi haggled a bit for two beers, one for himself and one for Cirtron. The little girls got their sodas. He paid four hundred "j" for the two beers and around seventy five "j" for each of the little girl's sodas. He had haggled a bit and got a decent deal considering it was the airport.

The tan Chevy Impala had been in the family for more than three generations. Basi was proud of the red license plate that the government of Jamaica had awarded him after his application was approved to allow him to be an "official" cab driver. Americans, of course, upon seeing the car, were a little apprehensive about riding with Basi because of the car's vintage. But, nonetheless, Basi earned a sort of living from being a cabby and was the only member of the family from the hills that did so. Cirtron was more than happy to see Basi and all of those in and on the car and was lucky to have the transportation.

Uncle Basi hugged Cirtron again as a greeting and as recognition of Cirtron's return.

Cirtron exclaimed, "Basi, my aunt! How be my aunt? Are you still be de treating her so?"

"Ya, mon. I be treating her so! Same as before. Ai! Ha! Where you b'en doing?"

"None so much. De car. She still to be alrigh' to be de go back home?"

"Irie! She be sound an' fit, mon.'

In the back of the car, with its sun-damaged plastic seats and dash, the little girls grasped their sodas, (a rare treat) and listened to the exchange between the two men. They were sure that Cirtron would have something for them. And of course, we knew that he did.

"Ahhh, little ladies. You be waiting de s'prise? Yes, mon?"

The response was not negative. The little girls all giggled and strained to lean out of the car's windows at once.

Cirtron unzipped the gym bag. His black hand, pink palm and long extended fingers produced Redstripe from the bag. Cirtron is not a big man, not in stature. But his hand was large enough to cradle Redstripe with his fingertips under her chest and the heel of his hand supporting her tummy. Redstripe's legs gripped nothing but air and paddled as if to swim to a more secure spot. Her little black eyes rolled back to show the whites for just a moment.

The little girls squealed with delight. Cirtron handed Redstripe through the back window (it had not had glass in it anyway for eight years) and into the collective laps of the little girls.

Basi said that they should go. "K' de bottles, mon. We t'in later, mon."

Once in the car, Redstripe busied herself with her newfound freedom, jumping from willing lap to willing lap, to shoulder and then arms and to the back seat ledge and everywhere. As Uncle Basi started the Chevy and drove off, the little girls began to pester Cirtron asking just what sort of creature Redstripe was.

Uncle Basi headed the old car away from the airport toward the mountains.

The way Uncle Basi took home was long, twisted and arduous. The old set of wheels bumped and wheezed down the dirt lanes.

Basi drove, in spite of the roads, like a driver doing the Indy 500. Most Jamaicans drive like this.

Norman Manley Boulevard, a road right near the airport, was paved. It was paved between the potholes in any event. But after all, the Jamaican concept of "road" is just a wide spot of mud or dirt (depending on the weather) dividing two groups of huts or trees. Actually, the goats of Jamaica are the real legitimate denizens of the roads, not cars. Once Basi left the boulevard, things got interesting.

Goats in Jamaica are indeed a hazard on the roads on the island. The first time the car bearing Cirtron and Basi and the little girls came across these bleating and hairy creatures, they got, well, Redstripe's "goat." There, it is said.

Goats do not understand that they should cooperate in any way with human beings. The first time a group of them blocked the progress of the old Chevy, Basi leaned out to shout while he leaned on his horn. Cirtron assisted with great animation and shouts as well. "Leave by de road, mon!" "Away, mon! Go, Gaahhh!"

Redstripe entered the fray with complete dachshund abandonment. The first time she "saw goat," there were three. They were big. Still, Redstripe was sure she could help clear the road of the goats. After all, the humans were shouting and gesticulating. Certainly she could help.

"Raaarrrrfff!" said Redstripe and then "RAAARRRFFF!" again. She jumped to the front seat and onto the dashboard. "Raaarrrfff!" In the language of dachshunds this means "goat! I see GOAT!"

In her excitement, one of her small paws hit the blinker control in the car. Then again, another of her paws hit the radio control as she scrambled to see the goats out of the front window. With Redstripe "raarrrfffing" and Cirtron and Basi shouting, the blinkers blinking and the radio hissing, the goats moved off. They presumably wanted calmer pastures.

Redstripe could barely wait for the next goat. She remained on the dashboard, shivering and shaking.

"Ahhh, little dog. Be still!" said Cirtron. "You no to be de mess wid de goat, mon. She have de teeth, keen?"

Redstripe did not "keen" at all. All she knew was that she needed to get just as close as possible to these hairy creatures. She was bound and determined to do just that. She vibrated with tension and her hackles roses up into a strip down her back. Basi saw this as he drove on and said, "Well, mon. De Redstripe, she has de red stripe! Ya, mon!"

The journey to Cirtron's home in the hills continued while Redstripe kept a look out for goats.

Redstripe did not starve as she rode along in the old Chevy as it bumped, bumbled and bustled down the back roads of the Jamaican hills. She didn't have a chance to starve. The little girls had plenty of food they all wanted to feed Redstripe in the back seat. The food was all wrapped in cloth by the aunts and mothers back home. Cirtron and Basi were oblivious to all of this feeding going on right behind them. But the aunts and mothers would not have been pleased to see that all of the food was going to the little dog and not the little girls. Eyebrows would be raised and brooms would swing. Redstripe, though, was happy to feed on bits of yam, carrot and greasy chicken.

Cirtron, of course, had saved a bread roll from the plane and that went to Redstripe too. Eventually, Redstripe, bloated and hot, settled down and snoozed off in the laps of the little girls. The little girls had worn themselves out as well and the whole pile of girls and puppy slept in the back seat of the Chevy; the sight of which would become quite common.

They approached Cirtron's home.

Redstripe's Dubious Arrival

From the air, one would see lush foliage and a few narrow paths following the ridges of the gently rounded mountains. A few steel roofs marred the sight, rusting in the moist air and baking in the relentless sun. From above, the oppressive humidity could not be felt there in the interior of the island. Nor could one hear the constant buzzing of insects nor smell the fecundity of the tropical jungle.

On the ground, a visitor would see the smaller huts, roofed with woven thatch that made up the sleeping quarters of the children. These were wooden-floored and were raised off of the jungle floor. The resulting space created an abode underneath for various chickens and pigs that dwelled in the relatively cool and shaded soil.

Several goats wandered about, and the chickens owned the place.

The old Chevy wheezed into the small group of huts and dwellings that Basi, Cirtron and the girls called home. Their approach had been heard from a long way off and all of the relatives were at hand and waiting anxiously. Not a whole lot happened there, up in the Jamaican Mountains. Cirtron was the prodigal son and his returns from his travels always held the promise of tales of mischief.

Amongst shouts and waves and cheers and squawking chickens and squealing pigs, the old Chevy let loose a hissing cloud of steam from its old and devastated radiator. The car rolled to a dusty stop. An inquisitive pig snuffled around the side of the car. Cirtron had arrived back home.

Redstripe woke up.

The crowd that had rushed the car stopped upon seeing Redstripe in the back seat. They were stone still. They had never seen a dachshund and had no idea what they were looking at there in the laps of the yawning little girls.

Someone pointed and asked, "Waht be dis?" and peered into the back seat with a worried look. Someone else, alarmed, said "de baby rat? Cirtron! Waht be you de bring ta here, mon?"

Another, "Ahh, y'find de pig, de baby pig!"

"No, mon! Never see de pig like so, mon! Too much hair!"

"Cirtron, mon. Ayie! *Wahd be dis?*"

Cirtron, cool as always, said, "No problem, mon. She be Redstripe, she be a dach—"

But it was too late. Redstripe smelled *pig!* And she leaped from the laps of the little girls, clambered out the open window and tumbled to the ground, feet scrambling for purchase in the dust as soon as she landed. The little girls burst from the doors, the snuffling pig, now alarmed, took off and the chase was on.

It was Redstripe in the lead, second only to the pig, paws a blur and ears flapping. Her tongue blew back out of the side of her jaws from the wind caused by her speed. Next was Cirtron. Then came the little girls who were followed by the shouting crowd. The men ran and waved and the women held up their long skirts as they chased after the dog and girls and Cirtron. Basi stayed and leaned on the car. He was way too smart for this nonsense. Not so for the pig.

The pig had never seen anything like this!

And it didn't like it. Not one bit.

Redstripe had arrived.

Interlude at Maddie's Bar, Negril

It may now be time to take a moment to describe just how we met Cirtron. After all, it is Cirtron who first told us this story. We met him late at night as we leaned up against the rail of one of the many bars that sit back from the edge of the beaches in Negril. There are countless numbers of these. And none are fancy. They are all "open air" and quite rough. Almost anything anyone wants can often be had. We have declined many offers over time.

Some of the bars do not even have refrigerators for beer. The operators rely on coolers and ice to keep things chilled. After the sun goes down, many travelers would not even go near the smaller places. But we pride ourselves in experiencing places avoided by the faint of heart. Drinking a tepid beer in the dark with strangers in another country may not be everyone's idea of a good time. We live for it. That's Jamaica. Those travelers who stay within the walls of their all-inclusive resorts are missing the whole point of the island. Cirtron's story is only one of many we have collected by the light of the Jamaican moon.

We stopped one night, during one of our walks, at a palm frond roofed hut called "Maddie's." The slow night waves washing on the beach and the stars glinting silently in the sky had lost their charm for a bit. Unbelievable, but one gets immune to the Jamaican beauty after a while. This can happen after a week or so. We turned away from the beach to approach Maddie's. You would not know it was Maddie's—there was no sign—you had to ask. But not right away, please. This is not polite. This would not demonstrate respect. All that was in the bar was a bartender, two rastamafarians, a cooler and a Coleman lantern that hung from a wire. The lantern hissed quietly and cast a pale yellow glow onto the scarred surface of the plywood bar.

"Ya, mon." said the woman behind the bar. She was huge. But she was well dressed for the situation; colorful dress and gold necklaces.

"Irie," we said back.

And we asked for two Redstripes, sixty "j."

Cirtron and Asha, brothers, we discovered later, were perched on rickety stools at the bar. They each bummed a smoke from us; a practice we came to understand was part of the price of the beer in many places. Cirtron was dutifully weaving a bracelet from green, yellow and black threads he held in a tangled pile on his lap. He sold bracelets like the one he was making on the beach. To watch him was wondrous. His long black fingers, with their contrasting pink nails flew as he manipulated the rolls of thread in his lap to the work at hand. How he did what he did in the dim light is still a mystery to us.

"Ahh, lady, be you de want de bracelet? I make you one, mon. I make you one."

"Well, I don't know," Jill said cautiously.

I glanced at another man, not seen at first, on the side of the little hut. He was holding a baseball bat and stood as though he meant to use it. Cirtron caught my eye.

"Ahh, mon. Not to worry, mon. He dere to watch for you! See, we love all de people day come by. See? Keen, mon. We want no one de bother you."

"I see."

"No, mon. Be it de truth, mon. You see. Go wid Ga, respect."

We began a long talk with Cirtron and Asha. And we agreed to pay Cirtron to weave bracelets for our kids with their names on them. The bracelets were woven in black, green, yellow and red over armatures cut from plastic milk bottles. The colors have certain meanings. The yellow and green are the sun and the earth. The red is the blood of the people. The black represents the joining of all cultures and people. From this comes the phrase that is so commonly used in Jamaica, "one people, one blood."

It took a while, but finally Cirtron made us feel at ease. So it was there in the shadows under the lantern in Maddie's bar, bat-equipped guard on hand, the ocean sighing in the distance, unseen, that Cirtron told us his story about Redstripe and Sheila. It was two years later, during a chance meeting with Cirtron at the same place that we heard the end of the story and it was completed.

Redstripe Settles In and Tastes Jamaican Cooking

Once Redstripe and Cirtron were settled into the village in the hills, the days came and went, one day pretty much like the one before it. The women spent most of their days tending the gardens. They grew yams, heavenly tomatoes, and carrots as the main crops. The men of the conclave spent most of their days being lazy. So it was with the men that Redstripe spent most of her time during the days.

The chickens and goats and pigs eventually came to an understanding with Redstripe. Redstripe would not chase them and in exchange the goats and pigs would not bite her. The chickens and Redstripe lost interest in each other and the chickens kept to themselves. Redstripe did end up with some scars that did heal on her head. If one would part the coat on her hindquarters, a small scar would be seen that had been caused by the teeth of a goat who had not been interested in being herded about by the likes of the little red dog. The goat made that clear.

At night, when it was time to really rest, Redstripe slept with the little girls in one of the raised wooden huts. The girls and Redstripe lay in heaps on the cots like piles of so many puppies snoozing during the cool nights in the mountains. Redstripe always found a way to insert herself warmly between two or more little bodies The mothers and aunts were not thrilled with this arrangement but finally gave up and let it go. Redstripe was then safe from the "brooms of discipline."

No one can visit Jamaica and not become acquainted with jerk sauce. This is the Jamaican equivalent of barbecue sauce but it can be unbelievably hot. Tomatoes (the heavenly ones), peppers onions and spices make up the sauce but the main bite comes from a small little pepper, a Chile-like fruit, called a Scotch Bonnet. Scotch Bonnet, Scottish Basket and Habenero are all names for this little wicked pepper.

These little peppers (they look like miniature yellow pumpkins) grow on a tall, bush-like plant. They are so hot, they cannot be handled safely with bare hands. Gloves of some kind must be worn when preparing them and only the cooking and cutting utensils can touch the raw ones. Rub one of their seeds between your fingers and just run your finger against your nose and you won't see a thing for half an hour. And that half an hour will be pure misery. Believe this. Been there and done that!

Yet, no one can resist the mouth-watering smell of this sauce when used while cooking pork or chicken or goat. When used as a sauce, the dish in which it is used becomes jerked chicken or jerked pork or jerked goat. Redstripe couldn't resist the smell either. She discovered the power of the Scotch Bonnets the hard way.

A pot of this jerk sauce, not fully cooked, but warm from the fire, was placed for a moment on a low bench. Redstripe, being a dachshund, just *had* to investigate.

It took only one lick and a noseful of the stuff. Redstripe rocketed off, shaking her head furiously, trying to rid herself of the sting. She ran this way and that, rubbed her head on the ground nearly hard enough to lose her hide and then pawed at her snout all the while making loud wooking noises. She dashed right. And then reversed and dashed left. She whirled. It was all to no avail.

She sneezed in reverse; a loud hoarse and painful sound. She sneezed again with such force she was knocked back unto her haunches. She was a mess. It *hurt*!

But one of the Jamaicans, being a Jamaican, knew what to do to rescue the little dog and end her discomfiture. Gently smiling and in good humor, he grabbed the little dog and held a bowl of goat's milk up to the poor little dog's nose.

But Redstripe wanted no part of that. She bucked away. She wanted nothing to do with goat and besides she could not think straight from the pain and did not understand that someone was only trying to help.

"Ahh, well, den, little dog. So, mon." said her helper. The Jamaican carried Redstripe over to a larger metal bucket of goat's milk. There was just enough to submerge a struggling and wriggling dachshund's little head. She was dunked once and came up snorting and flapping her ears like mad. Another dunk and she came up but sneezed a bit less violently. Three dunks and her benefactor could tell that the goat's milk was neutralizing the sting of the jerk sauce. Redstripe looked ridiculous with her white-soaked head in contrast with her red body. But she felt lots better.

"Ahhh, little dog," said her savior, "Not to be de drink de sauce, mon. Eeez too hot, mon. Too hot for de little dog."

Redstripe never, ever, went near anything "jerked" after that. But she'd walk a mile for some goat's milk.

Easter Monday

Anyone who visits Jamaica would notice that the Christian religion of the western world is held in high regard on the island. This may come as a surprise to visitors. After all, Jamaica has a very different culture than the culture of the North American or the European Continent. The existence of Christian worship on the island has, we think, something to do with the various peoples who, at one time or another during the last few centuries, have visited the island and left their marks, blood and influence. There have been French, British and African contributions that have all blended together with the original local culture. Of course, when it comes to religion on Jamaica, the women show a much greater interest in the theological teachings of Western Europe and North America than do the men.

This western Christian influence shows itself in at least two holidays. One is a "Mardi Gras" type celebration called "Carnival." The other is "Easter Monday." Easter Monday is named for the calendar date that it implies. It is always the Monday of the week just after Easter Sunday. Cirtron, Basi, the little girls and the rest of the family headed out of the mountains and into Negril for the holiday of Easter Monday. Redstripe was included, of course. The goats, chickens and pigs stayed behind. So did an uncle or two that never woke up early enough to make the trip.

Basi was really the only one of the group who had any reliable income at all. Cirtron made some money selling his bracelets and services, but, more often than not, very little of what Cirtron made came back to the village. Basi's money came from the fares he transported in the old tan Chevy around the resorts and hotels in Negril. He also made a bit of money from repairing small gasoline engines in a little hut he built for himself in the hills. Most often, the repairs he made were only completed when he managed to order parts. Sometimes it took a year before those parts he ordered came by mail so that he could fix the pumps and chain saws and other little engines that were brought to him.

Basi had enough mechanical knack to keep that old tan '69 Chevy going. The Chevy that had brought Cirtron and Redstripe home was the same transportation used by the group to get to Negril for Easter Monday. The food was packed. The little girls were stuffed into the back seat with Redstripe. The blankets and tents and relatives all were piled into and onto the car. Negril was the destination, then, for the Easter Monday holiday.

Once at Negril, after the trip down from cockpit country in the mountains, the group first piled off and out at Bloody Bay. The bay was named centuries ago for the slaughtering of whales that were brought up into its shallow waters. Booby Cay, a small island, lies just off shore. It is not really within swimming distance and is guarded by jellyfish. But it is just a small haul for the fish vendors that hunt the reefs nearby with their carved canoes and then hawk their catches on the beach. There, at Bloody Bay, at the public park, the adults set down their food bags and tents just north of the main area.

Everyone crammed back into and onto Uncle Basi's old Chevy and Uncle Basi pulled out of the park and aimed the car toward the more populated stretches of the seven miles of Negril Beach.

Redstripe would soon learn all about crabs

Basi's car lumbered down the narrow strip of asphalt road that ran parallel to the seven miles of beach in Negril. Various resorts and other establishments separated the road from the beach. Grand Lido, Hedonism II, Sandals, Yellow Bird and the Tree House all passed by on the right side of the road as the group continued. They stopped at about mid-beach and pulled into the parking lot at Alfred's, the very-Jamaican beachfront restaurant and bar that would be their passage to the beach. Cirtron was well known at Alfred's.

Everyone piled out. Redstripe was carried in the arms of one of the little girls and the little dog sniffed and snorted at the smell of grilling lobsters in the shell. She could also smell conch being grilled over open coals. The smell of jerk sauce was in the air as well, but Redstripe knew better than to become interested in that aroma. The women and little girls, with Redstripe, headed for the beach. The men headed for the bar "Ya, mon. De rum, mon!"

Alfred's is just about in the middle of the beach that starts in Negril Village and ends seven miles later to the north at the high priced resorts near Booby Cay. On Easter Monday, the entire stretch is filled with people. The water is nearly obliterated by bodies in the ocean, frolicking and just having a good old time in the warm waters and sun of the Caribbean. Hawkers roam the beach selling bracelets, fresh fish and lobster, juice and fruit. Jamaican entrepreneurs entreat the crowd to parasail or to rent jet-skis. The place is pure pandemonium. And everyone has a great time on Easter Monday.

Redstripe could not get enough of the excitement. She ran back and forth on the beach and then toward the water, challenging the waves, getting an occasional unplanned dousing of salt water after a miscalculated lunge. She trotted after those walking along and hawking their goods and did a great job of being a general nuisance to everyone in sight.

Sand coated her. She was a mess of wet fur, beach sand and smelly dead things she had found to play with. Now and again, one of the little girls would carry her into the ocean and dunk her clean. The girls would shriek and shout as Redstripe was encouraged to paddle about in the water, her eyes pulled back and showing their whites. The girls would pluck her from the water and then deposit the little dog back on the sand where she would proceed to get just as filthy as possible all over again, scampering and rolling until every last inch of her reddish fur was covered with sand and slop.

The beaches of Negril, if one would take a close look on a day when there are not a lot of people around, are dotted here and there with little dime sized-holes; the homes of small crabs that are about the same size as the holes. To Redstripe, the smell in those holes was absolutely irresistible. Sniff, *sniff*! Snort, *snort*! Dig and dig and *dig*! Redstripe just had to get to one of those little crabs and was digging like crazy. In our house, we like the phrase, "Don't wish too hard for something, you might get it."

Redstripe got her wish.

Excavating like mad, Redstripe's long body was halfway down into the sand when she found a crab. It made a good try to scuttle away up the hole that the dog had dug but it was just too slow for the determined little dachshund. Little jaws snapped, nearly closing on the hapless crustacean. It backed away sideways just as quickly as it could manage and then lifted up one small claw toward the menacing little hound and clamped onto a soft, velvety ear.

Yipe! Shake! Yipe! This had not been in the plans. Redstripe whirled about and headed for the water, plunging, paws forward, in a panic. The crab still clung to her ear. Once in the water, the crab let go; meandering off to do whatever it is that crabs do in crab land. And no one really knows what that might be.

Redstripe clambered out of the water and back onto the sand. She shook off the saltwater, ears flapping, and plunked down. She looked up as if to say, "Crab? What crab? I didn't see a crab."

But she dug no more holes that day.

The Easter Monday holiday for all of the aunts and uncles and children passed by in Negril. The men spent the days trying to sell this and that on the beach. They sold bracelets they had woven (not as good as Cirtron's) and packs of cigarettes they hauled about in netted bags. The women and the children spent their time splashing about in the warm ocean waters and sitting on the sand in the sun. Redstripe eventually just tired herself out and deposited herself down in the shade of an aloe bush. These aloe bushes grow to be more than six feet tall and the lush leaves are broken off by hand. The thick leaves are then split to release a jell that can be rubbed onto the sun bruised skins of the tourists who chose not to heed the warnings about he Caribbean sun and its power.

By Tuesday, the seven miles of the white sands of the beaches of Negril were deserted. The Jamaicans all headed back home and the tourists boarded the chartered busses to travel back over the goat strewn roads to Montego Bay and the airport there. Uncle Basi, Redstripe and the family gathered at the camp at Bloody Bay and prepared for the trip back to their home in the mountains.

Cirtron had made other plans.

"Basi," said Cirtron. "I made de call to ma friend back, she be, in New York. I not to be de go back t' home jus' now, mon. You go ahead wid de family."

Basi said, "Ya not to be no good, mon. We be ready to leave, mon. Up witch you!"

Cirtron continued, "Well, ah, y'see, mon. I make de call to de lady and she be wanting de visit, once more, mon. I used de collect, d'y see, mon?"

Basi sighed. There was no reasoning with Cirtron. There never had been. Cirtron had snuck off during the holiday to make a collect call to Sheila in New York. She had promised him another airline ticket and wanted to see him once again. Redstripe, of course, was invited. Sheila had been happy to take Cirtron's collect call. She wanted dearly to see the little Redstripe once again. Cirtron was part of the deal.

Basi and the family headed for the hills in the old Chevy. Redstripe was deposited in her now-normal means of conveyance, the gym bag. The Chevy rumbled off in one direction and Cirtron, Redstripe in the bag over his shoulder, held his thumb out for a ride in the other. Montego Bay Airport was the destination for the Rasta Man and the little red dog. This time, things would not go as smooth at the airport.

Return to Mo-Bay

Cirtron and Redstripe made their way from Negril to Montego Bay by thumb, foot and paw. The rest of the family made their way back to their home in the hills. It took a few days for the man and little dog to bum rides to the airport in Mo-Bay. Cirtron shamelessly used Redstripe to get people to stop. It was hard to turn Cirtron down with Redstripe panting in his arms in the Caribbean sun.

They walked at times. They rode at times. Once in a while, Redstripe would faithfully trot along on her own four feet beside Cirtron, watching out for goats. Usually, she spent the trip riding in the gym bag, head out, sphinx-like, and sniffing the smells of Jamaican countryside. For the most part, Redstripe held the day. Cirtron stopped frequently where his credit was still somewhat accepted and Redstripe was always assured of some scraps from the back of somewhere. The little dog did not go hungry and Cirtron did not go thirsty. The proprietors were quick with food and water for the little dog. Cirtron got scraps and beer as an afterthought. He told stories not so much as payment, but rather as a distraction to the settling of the tabs.

It rained once each of the days of the three-day trek. Twice, they were lucky enough to be inside a bar or car. But once they were caught in the warm and windy rains of the afternoon Jamaican Caribbean climate. Cirtron was soaked but he dried later in the sun. Redstripe was not so lucky to get dry. The gym bag filled with water and they had to stop for a while to empty Redstripe's little traveling bag and let it dry. Redstripe and Cirtron slept under a tree during this. Passers by just ignored the rasta man and the snoozing little dog. The two of them didn't really smell all that pleasant, anyway.

The two continued, begging, riding and walking along the coast road; Norman Manley Boulevard. Redstripe was happy to ride in the old cars that picked them up and just as happy to ride along in the gym bag, swinging against Cirtron's hip as he made his unhurried way to Montego Bay. From the neck down, Cirtron appearance was that of any black man in an urban area of the states. He had on the new jeans from Sheila and a somewhat fresh shirt. From the neck up, his beard and dreadlocks stated his origins.

Finally, after three days and some adventures to be told in a later story, the black man and the little red dog arrived at the Mo-Bay airport. They were both a bit scruffy so Cirtron hauled the gym bag into the men's restroom. Redstripe got sort of a bath in the sink. It was not a happy process at all. Others visiting the restroom cast strange glances at the man holding the strange little animal under the faucet. But this was Jamaica and no one created a fuss. Cirtron did what he could for himself.

A ticket, again paid for by Sheila, awaited them at the Trans Am desk. Cirtron proudly showed his passport and received his boarding pass and seat assignment. Redstripe was in the black gym bag, zipped in securely and asleep after the indignity and rigors of bathing in a restroom sink.

Cirtron, Redstripe a sling, left the confines of the terminal when the flight was called and made his was out over the tarmac to the huge jet. He clambered the metal and somewhat rickety stairs to board the plane.

New York lay ahead. And things would be a bit dicey on the return trip.

Flight to New York

Cirtron boarded the plane with Redstripe ensconced in the gym bag from Sheila. There were no questions about Cirtron's carry-on. They were lucky at that point, anyway. Once on the plane, Redstripe's bag was deposited safely under Cirtron's seat. Cirtron took a nap and he snored. Loudly. After all, he had been traveling

for three days and both the Jamaican and the little dachshund were
dog dead tired.

Redstripe, asleep (mostly) in the gym bag beneath Cirtron's seat,
heard the snorts and fluttering sounds from Cirtron as he slept.
She had heard enough of these in the mountains and on the trip
to Montego Bay to know what those sounds meant and she was
not alarmed. She settled down in the confines of the black gym bag,
secure and warm in the spot beneath Cirtron's seat.

After about an hour and a half into the flight, Cirtron woke up.
He needed to make a trip to the washroom. He hesitated. He did
not want to leave Redstripe in the bag beneath the seat while he
took care of business. So he gently wrested the gym bag out from
under his seat and slung the bag and little dog over his shoulder
once more. He headed for the front of the plane. No one really took
notice. It was not unusual for anyone to take carry-on luggage into
the washrooms on the planes so that they could use the contents
to freshen up or change clothes. All was calm. No one remarked
on the rasta man's passage.

Cirtron made his way into the washroom, locked the door after
some effort, and deposited the black gym bag on the small counter.
It took a while, but Cirtron finally puzzled out the instructions for
the toilet. He found the "flush" button and watched in amazement
as the blue water swirled around noisily to clean and hiss its way
out of the bottom of the "head."

It was loud. Very loud. And Redstripe barked out in concern from
her bag that was settled on the counter in the small washroom.

"Rarrf?" (What was THAT?!) "Rarrf!"

Cirtron tried to calm the little hound. "Shsssss, little dog. No to
be de get us in de trouble, mon! Jus' be de water, mon. Eezz alrigh',
mon. Be still, Irie."

Just outside the washroom, in the galley, two flight attendants were straightening things. They heard Redstripe bark. They looked at each other in surprise and went to listen outside of the washroom door.

Cirtron opened the door to the washroom to see two very pretty and yet sternfaced young ladies, their arms crossed . One asked, " Sir? What is going on here? We heard a dog bark. What is this?"

"Ahhh, ladies. Ahhh, eeezz jus a ..." Cirtron paused. He sensed that 'A chile of god' would not work here.

"Dog? Haa, Haa! No, mon! Dog? No. Not you be to find de dog here. Eez me, mon, d'you see? I have de cough. Carrphg! Carrphg! Have de little cough, mon. No dog, mon. Haa, Haa! D'y'see? Carrphg!"

The flight attendants were not convinced, but they let Cirtron return to his seat with his bag and hidden dog unmolested for a time.

Of the two attendants, the senior flight attendant was not convinced. Not to be outdone, she entered the flight deck to speak with the captain. She asked for his support. It seemed one of those *Jamaicans* had a small animal in a bag. They needed to get to the bottom of it, and right now! The captain wearily followed the two flight attendants and headed back to the passenger cabin to confront Cirtron. The youngest lady was in the lead, followed by the senior attendant. The captain brought up the rear.

The aisles, even on big jets, are narrow, of course and it is only possible to pass single file. When the group of investigators reached Cirtron's assigned seat, only the first person, the least senior flight attendant, could actually get right abreast of Cirtron. He was in the window seat and she had to lean over to get his attention.

"Sir? Excuse me, sir?" said the captain from two seats ahead of Cirtron. "We have to ask you to open that bag you have under your seat, sir. There seems to be a problem."

Cirtron froze. Nothing creative came to his mind. This was real bad.

As his hands trembled slightly and a glean of sweat popped out on his forehead, he pulled Redstripe's traveling bag from under his seat. He slowly unzipped the bag, his eyes closed and expecting the worst. The captain and the older attendant could not see from where they stood. The younger attendant peered down into the gym bag.

Up gazed the little red dog, ready and waiting to meet another new friend. She had just woken up, really, and her little black eyes focused on the pretty girl. "Another friend?" she thought. "Oh, good! Maybe she has *food!*" Redstripe waited in gleeful anticipation. Her front paws pedaled up and down in excitement.

The flight attendant was stunned. "Uh!" she said. "Oh my! Well, um, gee!"

"Well, what is it?" said the captain, impatience clear in his voice.

Redstripe looked up at the attendant and then to Cirtron. Cirtron opened his eyes and gave his best baleful look to the attendant. The girl looked at Cirtron and then back down at Redstripe. She did not know what to do. But her heart did.

She looked Cirtron in the eye and said, "Sorry, sir. We've made a mistake. We apologize. You know, we have to be very careful for the safety of all the passengers on our flights. Sometimes we need to check things for everyone's benefit."

"Ya, mon. Irie!" (whew!)

"Captain? There is nothing here to be concerned about. Sorry."

"Honestly," said the captain. "Sir," he addressed Cirtron, "Please accept my apology on behalf of Trans Caribbean. Enjoy the rest of your flight, please. If there is anything you require, please let the attendants know." He turned on his heel, and harrumphed back to the flight deck, shaking his head.

The younger attendant turned to her senior and said, "Do you think the captain is mad?"

"Guess the guy really has a cough. Go figure!"

Cirtron closed the zip on the gym bag in a blink and no one bothered him the rest of the flight. But, funny, there was an extra tuna sandwich on Cirtron's tray when it was time for lunch.

Drug Sniffing Dogs

Now that the crisis of a possible discovery of the smuggled little red dog was over, Redstripe and Cirtron settled down for the rest of the flight back from Jamaica. Both of them were full of tuna sandwich. The man next to them, on the aisle seat, had chosen a meal of Salisbury steak for himself. It had interested the all-knowing nose of Redstripe for a bit, but the tuna had sufficed.

Well, mostly it had sufficed.

Cirtron's seat partner had spilled some of the gravy from the Salisbury Steak onto the lower leg of his pants. Redstripe stuck her head out of the bag from under the seat to take a preliminary and desultory sniff. Cirtron admonished the little dog to be still and behave. The seat partner was just a little irritated. But for some reason he did not want to cause attention to himself and let the incident go. Cirtron and Redstripe were still safe.

The plane, bearing Cirtron, Redstripe and the Salisbury Steak guy, dropped down and out of the upper regions of the sky over the eastern coast of the United States and it banked to make a final approach to the airport. Cirtron, bag and dog in lap (which was against the airline rules... all carryons need to be beneath your seat or in the overhead compartments), waited for the landing. The wheels chucked down and the pilot made his final flare. The big jet touched down. First one wheel hit and screeched and then the others. Thump, thump..whirrr. They were down and safely back in New York.

Customs lay ahead. And in the United States, things are different and less "tolerant" for incoming visitors than in Jamaica.

Cirtron, dog in bag on shoulder, found himself in a long line. There were people there with all kinds of luggage. They had bags and cardboard cartons tied with twine. They had duffel bags and they had suitcases that bulged from poor packing. Long items suggested golf clubs, narrower ones suggested skis. Who knew what was in all of this stuff?

Cirtron waited and shuffled forward as the officials checked and asked questions. Cirtron waited some more. Redstripe was getting restless in the confines of the gym bag.

The Drug Enforcement Agency men were there among the lined-up passengers. The men and women of the agency all had dogs. The dogs were there as they had been trained to sniff about for things that should not be allowed to come into the United States. One particular dog, a seventy five-pound golden retriever named Shadow, was there with his trainer-agent.

Shadow was not, as his golden retriever ancestry might suggest, the calmest of dogs. But he loved to smell things. He had been trained to smell for things that were not appropriate to bring into the United States. His trainer-agent had no clue that Shadow just liked to smell things and wanted to smell everything. Shadow did not just want to smell the scents he had been trained to find during his time in the DEA facilities in Vermont. He just wanted to smell everything.

As Cirtron stood in line, he took a chance. He opened the gym bag's zipper a bit to let Redstripe have some fresh air. Cirtron noticed that the man from the aisle seat, the one with the spilled gravy on his lower pant leg, was just in front in line.

Shadow was sniffing around the arriving passengers just a few yards away. Redstripe looked up and out of the open bag, craning her neck to see the sights. Without warning she took a leap up and out her little cradle and hit the floor running. She streaked over the tiles to head for the big golden retriever. "Another new friend to meet!" thought Redstripe.

"Ahh! No! y'little dog. AIE, mon! Get y'back ya little dog!"

It was too late. The people waiting in lines began to stir and notice the dachshund galloping toward Shadow.

She sprinted right up to the big dog as fast as she could pump her little legs. Shadow's agent looked down at the dachshund and held tight to Shadow's leash. But he could not prevent the big dog from lowering his shoulders and sniffing the little red creature that seemed to have appeared from nowhere. Shadow sniffed and snorted and gave a loud "*Wuff!*"

It sent Redstripe backpedaling as fast as she could. She wheeled around and scampered back to the line where she had been in the bag with the waiting Cirtron. Shadow had a new smell to pursue; Redstripe. And his paws scrabbled on the tile in pursuit of the little hound; the adult in charge of him in tow.

Well.

Redstripe got back to Cirtron's line. Shadow was following but Redstripe had already forgotten about the golden. She did smell Salisbury Steak. And she quickly found the source of that smell on the cuff of the passenger that had been on the plane next to Cirtron. The man with the smelly cuff was standing in line for the customs check.

Her jaws clamped down on the savory cuff.

Shadow skidded up to the encounter.

The rest of the DEA agents in the airport, heretofore undercover, descended on the area to see what was going on. Their guns were not drawn, but lots of hands hovered over holstered weapons. It became absolute bedlam. Shadow jumped into the fray and knocked over the Salisbury Steak guy. Redstripe hung on to the guy's cuff, growling and readjusting her jaws, hanging on for dear life. Agents came from everywhere. They were rudely jostling through the travelers and pushing over luggage to get to the two dogs. Some cases fell over and fell open, spilling their contents among some of the people who were already down on the floor. Cirtron was among them.

He scrambled on his hands and knees to try to reach Redstripe. There were people and bags and clothes and dogs and everything in a tangle. Cirtron could not quite get to Redstripe. People were yelling, the dogs were barking and growling, the agents were shouting and all the non-involved people nearby seemingly descended on the mess.

Redstripe, Shadow and Cirtron looked up and paused. "Who? Us? We were just having fun." Cirtron smiled one of his smiles. But the DEA agents looked down on the floor to see something that had fallen out of the pocket of the Salisbury Steak man. It was something he should not have been carrying. Not at all.

After all were untangled, Cirtron was arrested. Redstripe was impounded at the airport. The man with the gravy stained cuff was arrested as well and taken away. The evidence from his pocket was in the hands of the men from DEA.

But there was some real confusion.

The men from DEA had no inkling that Shadow wouldn't smell out contraband if his life depended on it. The training had not taken. What the DEA men did think, however, was that Redstripe somehow was able to do what Shadow had not. They didn't have a clue that Redstripe had "cuffed" the passenger because of the Salisbury Steak gravy and not because she smelled what had been in the little bag the passenger was carrying. Cirtron took advantage of this confusion.

When the DEA men questioned Cirtron he said, "Ahh, she eez a good dog, mon. Was raised by ma good friend, Sheila. Here she be in New Yark, mon. Sheila!"

"Who is this Sheila?" the men asked. "Where can we find her? Is she a dog trainer? Does she work for the government?"

"Ahh, no mon! Not for me to be de say, mon. But I know, see, de Redstripe has de mother, mon. She be Paris. Sheila, she be de tell you, mon."

Somehow, by some dark method available to the American government, Sheila was found by the men from DEA. Sheila was called to the airport and Cirtron was released to her. But Redstripe was transported to a facility in Vermont run by the DEA to be studied by scientists employed by the government. They worked on improving airport security. The little red dog would fascinate them.

Redstripe would make them earn their money while she was there.

Back at Maddie's

On an undermined date, sometime in April of 1995, we were back in Maddie's Bar. The only ones there were us, Cirtron and Maddie. Maddie had made some improvements. The Coleman lantern was gone and had been replaced by a single electric light bulb hanging on wires from the roof of the place. Progress goes on relentlessly, even in Jamaica.

"And then, Cirtron? I asked.

"Cirtron, what happened to Redstripe?" asked Jill. "How did you get away from the DEA guys ?"

Cirtron had paused. His black eyes with their yellowish whites gleamed in the darkness and reflected twin bright spots from the electric bulb. "Ahh, well. She came to be de oh kay. Irie." He grinned. "All de talk, mon. I have de tirst, mon!"

I motioned to Maddie for another Redstripe. Bottle in hand, Cirtron continued while I paid for the beer.

"Well, mon, see, de govmint men, day keep de Redstripe a while in dere mountains. I stay wid Sheila. De phone, mon. De phone she be de ringing all de time, mon. Sheila, she say day be studying de little dog. I dunno what day be want wid de little dog but Sheila, she say day be doing de tests. Day be tests for de smell, mon."

"When day speak wid me at de airport, mon, day ask me de questions. Ahh, like where de little dog be come from and how she come to be in de bag. Day had many of de questions, mon. I dunno how to be de answer for them and day had not patience, mon. They had no respect."

"Respect!" I said and brushed the knuckles of my closed fist with Cirtron's. Anyone, one, with any sense, learns this gesture when in Jamaica. It paves the way out of a lot of misunderstandings. This time, it was used just to get Cirtron to go on with his tale.

Cirtron took a long swallow of beer. The liquid's passage showed down Cirtron's skinny neck; a passing bulge like a snake swallowing a little rat. "Irie!" said Cirtron. "'Couple days, day be de bring back de little dog to Sheila. De mother ? Paris ? She be de know de little dog once more and day be happy back together. De mother, she be Paris, mon."

"We remember," I said. "But what did the men from the government say, Cirtron?"

"I don't know so. Day be talk to Sheila. She say day be ass—, uh, day be people wid no respect."

Indeed, by phone, Sheila had many conversations with the men from DEA. They were insistent that Redstripe must have some innate ability to smell things not wanted in airports. But they were frustrated and felt that Sheila had some clue why Redstripe would not perform at the facility in Vermont. Redstripe was gleefully uncooperative, as only dachshunds can be, and was wearing the scientists to a frazzle.

They gave up.

If only they had asked Redstripe to find Salisbury Steak. Or maybe jerk sauce would have brought a reaction. But being men of little vision, they were unsuccessful in turning the little dachshund into a drug-sniffer. So, after two days, Redstripe was returned to Sheila in the little apartment. The notes and files of observations of the little red dog were kept in a place with other seemingly-important secrets.

The men came in long black cars. When they got out onto the street in front of Sheila's apartment, their coats all bulged slightly over unseen things. They climbed the flights of stairs and handed Redstripe over to Cirtron at Sheila's apartment door.

"Sorry to have troubled you," one of them said in a tone that was insincere. "This has been a matter of international security. You understand this as an American, ma'am. Here is your dog."

Cirtron responded. "No problem, mon. She be de good, little dog, mon. You see?" Redstripe stretched up from where she lay cradled in Cirtron's arm and licked his neck through his beard. "You see, mon? Keen? She be a fine chile of ga!"

The men were not amused. One said, "We will be in touch when the dog has puppies. We will want to see them, of course."

"Not on your life, buddy," said Sheila over Cirtron's shoulder. "You guys have no respect!"

"Ahh, Sheila, Irie. I tink day be go now, be it oh kay." He looked at the men and raised an eyebrow. "Irie?"

"Yeah, sure. See you. We'll be in touch," they said. Then they all turned, stomped down the stairs and piled back into the black cars to leave.

All was then right with the world. Sheila was glad to have Cirtron visit once again and Cirtron was exited to see and take in the complicated sights and sounds of a city in the United States. Redstripe spent most of the time tussling and teasing with her mom. The two of the dogs, Paris and her little daughter, Redstripe, threatened major damage to the little apartment while Sheila and Cirtron would look on, laughing at the doggy antics.

In the back of her mind, Sheila remembered what the men from the DEA had said. They were interested in pups should Redstripe ever have any. Well, she would certainly see about *that*! But, for now, Redstripe was back in New York and Sheila and Cirtron agreed that she should stay there. After all, a busy rastamafarian's style might be a bit cramped trying to eek out a living *and* care for a dachshund back in Jamaica.

Cirtron returned to Jamaica.

When he left, the apartment held just Paris, Sheila and Redstripe. The only problem left was fitting the three of them comfortably under the same bedcovers at night. Generally, it was Sheila who ended up cold.

BERNARD

WE HAD BEEN SUSPICIOUS for a week or so. When we'd returned from a Friday night fish fry, the cushions on the living room couch had been in disarray. It hadn't been a big deal, but we noticed it. We went out other evenings. One night, all of the dog toys were strewn about the "office" in the basement. This was not something that Belle (our dachshund) would do. But we let that go. Then we noticed that throw rugs near the doors had been pushed about and were not there for our wet feet.

Later, when we returned home from some shopping trip or other, we noticed that Belle did not jump up to greet us. She was tired. Very tired. But we did not get overly concerned about that. We just felt she was just snoozing away and waiting for us to return. To wake up, it seemed to us, was just too much effort for the little dog. Generally, after we had been gone during the evening, we sent Belle out to "take care of things" and then brought her in, gave her the obligatory cookie and allowed her to wrap her self down among the covers in our bed to be warm and sleep for the rest of the night.

We were wrong about all of it. Little did we know.

The mussed cushions and rugs and Belle's energy level had an explanation. But it was not until Christmas Day that we understood.

Early on Christmas Eve, son Jeremy appeared, snaking and sliding his car up the drive. We had to get the shovel out to scrape out a semi-dry section of driveway for his wheels to grab. He made it up and then offered to help shovel the rest of the drive. While we were both out there, a dachshund appeared. It was snowing. It was cold. So we were surprised at the sight of this standard-sized dachs we had never seen before. The little dog bristled and barked at us when we tried to approach. His teeth were bared and he looked as though he would take a piece out of anyone who tried to get close.

We kept our distance and he wheeled and disappeared into the snowy night. Belle was inside making howling sounds and barking and snorting like a rabid animal.

"What was *that* all about?"

"Dad, forget it, it's a stray."

"It can't be. It's a dachshund for Pete's sake. He just must have got loose. I hope he is all right. I'm going to look for him."

"Yeah, right, Dad. Like you're going to find him at night," said Jeremy. "I'm going in. You have anything to eat inside?"

Jeremy was right. I could find no tracks in the frozen street beyond the driveway. I returned to the house, stomped off my feet, and joined everyone in the warmth of Christmas Eve. The kids were busy grazing on the cheese and crackers, herring, pizza, chips and dips that I had set out on the kitchen table. Belle had her own little platter of neat treats on the floor. She hadn't touched it.

"What was all that about?" Jill asked. "Belle has been going nuts! She has been barking like a banshee and can't settle down."

I explained, "Well, there was this dachshund out at the end of the drive that showed up while we were shoveling. He was acting really aggressive and then he ran off. I looked for him, but, well, I dunno. Belle must have heard him."

"Do you know where he went?" asked Jill.

"No, I have no clue, we'll have to watch for him. I expect he may be from a new family that just moved into the neighborhood. I've never seen him before. I hope he's okay, but I don't know what else I can do."

Jeremy called to me from the kitchen, "Hey, Dad, do we have any more soda?"

"Uh, yeah, it isn't cold, but you can get a twelve pack out of the basement. It should be down near the laundry."

Jeremy pounded down the stairs and then called, "Dad?! Come down here, you gotta look at something."

Down in the basement, near the laundry, a window was open. It was not open very much, it was open just a crack. And from that window was a trail of wet dirt and melting snow. It started on the sill of the window, went down to a shelf, onto the dryer and then onto the clothes table and then to a trunk near the table and onto the floor.

"Dad, some animal has been in here. I can see where it went! Take a look."

Several other trails had dried there. Something had been coming and going for some time. I thought a dachshund could have made that trip from sill to shelf to dryer to table to trunk and floor, but I didn't say anything.

Instead, "Jeremy, go on upstairs, I need to fix this window, it must not be locking right."

I reached up to lock the basement window. The latch would not engage and I bruised my knuckles trying to force the window latch into its receiver. I just couldn't do it. The window frame was a bit sprung and would not close all the way.

"Hell and damnation, I don't need this on Christmas Eve!" I shouted to no one in the basement.

I tried one more time to close the window and I was shocked.

A set of claws suddenly attacked the basement window from the outside. A set of teeth appeared outside the window in the darkness. They really looked nasty. I stumbled back and fell away from the window and onto the concrete floor.

"Whoa !!! Hey, geez. What *was that!*"

Later, we would come to know that those claws and teeth belonged to Bernard.

I went back upstairs and joined everyone. "Jeremy, that dog was here again! He was right at the basement window. I thought he was going to have my head for a snack. He was wild! I think it must have been him that came in the basement window. And I couldn't get it closed completely, the latch is broken."

Jill said, "You mean the dachshund you saw when you were shoveling? Is he okay? Where'd he go? God, I hate to think of him outside like that."

"He's a stray, Dad, like I said. Don't sweat it, hey?" Jeremy said.

Jill turned to Jeremy, "Don't you care? That dog must be lost or loose. He could freeze out there. It's Christmas; have some heart, would you?"

Jeremy shrugged and slugged his soda. Belle began to bark. I went to bandage my knuckles.

None of us really could think of anything to do about the mysterious dog. I silently decided to make regular checks out the windows and particularly the basement window throughout the evening. But things settled down into the traditions of Christmas.

We ate food and opened presents, and the phone took and sent calls from and to relatives in far-away places. Tree lights and the company of family created the peace we all needed during the season. Daughter Kaylie retired upstairs with her stepsister to do what ever it is that teenage girls do behind closed doors. Jill curled up to watch television with Belle and Jeremy and I went down to computer games in the office. Belle never did eat her treats.

Around 11 o'clock on Christmas Eve, most of us were ready for bed. Except for Jeremy, of course. He was glued to the computer. The rest of us went to bed. But the peace that is supposed to come with Christmas Eve was just not going to be available.

Most of us had been in bed for around an hour. Midnight had passed and Jeremy was the only one up. The computer was bleeping and running cool graphics and doing what computers do when running computer games. But Jeremy heard something else. It was coming from the back of the basement, back in the laundry. Over the sound from the computer speakers, he heard thumping and scratching from the back room.

"What?"

Jeremy rose from his chair at the computer desk and went to look. He opened the door to the laundry. It was dark and he reached for a light switch and when the light came on a cacophony of barking and snarling began instantaneously. Jeremy slammed the door and ran upstairs to wake me.

"Dad! Dad! Hey, Dad! It's *back!*"

"Uh.. what ..? Oh, I hear it, what *is* that?" I was not in my most alert state.

"Dad, it's the dog again, it's in the basement. It was about to attack me, for cripes sake! You gotta come downstairs!"

That seemed reasonable to me., "All right already, I'm coming."

Jill woke, "What is going on?"

Jeremy and I raced down the stairs. Well, Jeremy raced. I stumbled. And we came to the laundry room door. By that time, all was quiet. Jill had made her way slowly down and no one noticed that Belle was in tow as well. I put my hand on the doorknob and turned it.

With Jeremy peering over my shoulder, I pulled open the door. And the barking and snarling began again. It was the dachshund.

He was right there with something brown with a little green at his feet.

He barked and backed and snarled dangerously.

I thought for just a second, "Jeremy, see if you can't grab one of those dirty towels in the pile near the washer, I'll try to get to him, but I'll need the towel to grab him so I don't get bitten."

Jeremy looked at me like I was crazy, but then he began to inch toward the dirty laundry. The dog kept barking and snarling and I still could not concentrate on what he had there on the floor long enough to make it out. No one noticed that Belle had entered the room. She padded straight to the strange dog and stopped. So did he.

"Belle, *no!*" It was a chorus.

The two dachshunds licked noses and sniffed ears, as we all stood there, stunned. In the back of my mind, I now knew what had been messing up things in the house recently. Mystery explained. This ol' dachshund had been sneaking in to see our Belle and they had been having a good ol' time while we were gone!

We stood there, still frozen, and Kaylie wandered in. "Hey, what is... oh, how *cute!* And he brought Belle a present! Cool!"

As the two dogs continued to sniff and lick, I asked Kaylie, "Present? What present?"

"Well look, silly, the dog even wrapped it for Belle. 'Course you don't have your glasses on."

Okay, I looked. And I finally got a good look at the brown and green thing on the floor. It was what was left of a pork chop with a piece of green Christmas ribbon sort of stuck to it.

The dog, turned, picked it up in his jaws and then dropped it at Belle's feet. I said, "Kaylie, that's some trash that was probably mixed in with Christmas wrappings and he dragged it in here to eat."

"Dad, it's a present for Belle." Kaylie was emphatic.

Belle certainly thought so. She lay down on the concrete, grabbed the thing in her two front paws and began to chew on the decimated chop as the mystery dog looked on. None of us quite knew what to do, but I approached the unnamed hound and bent down with a hand out. He didn't flinch and he allowed me to scratch his neck while Belle continued to chew on the chop.

While scratching him, I said, "Boy, is this guy thin. He must have been out there for a while. Where in the world did he come from? *Someone* must be missing him."

The group descended on the dog while Belle continued to gnaw.

"Hey, little guy, where do you belong?"

"Are you cold? Are you hungry?"

"Hey, we've got leftovers, you want some?"

"Oh, you poor guy, your ribs are showing!"

The dog had dropped his aggressive demeanor and welcomed the attention. We dried him off, got him water and some food and a blanket. We planned to let him sleep down in the basement for the night but when we closed the door, Belle let us know that this was not going to be. He was not to be alone unless we wanted the laundry room door scratched into splinters by Belle. They ended up in the same blanket that night. That was after I put a nail through the casement of the basement window to secure it.

Two o'clock in the morning found us around the kitchen table. It was too early for coffee and too late for any libations for the two adults. We settled on hot cider for everyone. The question was what to do.

"Dad," said Kaylie, "he has to be around from somewhere here. Let's go knock on doors, we can split up the streets."

Jill said, "Uh, I don't think so. First, no one wants to be wakened on Christmas morning at this early an hour and, well, what if someone thinks we're Santa Claus and is disappointed?"

"Santa Claus comes down chimneys, Jill," said Jeremy. "Last time I heard, he doesn't knock. But how about if I go and hit the all night grocery stores and see if there is a lost dog notice on the bulletin boards?"

"Can I go with you?" Kaylie begged.

"I suppose. I'll drive, you look."

The kids took off into the night and I sat at the table with Jill, drumming my fingers. "I have an idea, but it's a long shot. I suspect that dog downstairs has been out and around for a week or so. That's why there are multiple tracks from the basement window that didn't close and why things have been out of place around here. Belle and this guy have been, well, who knows what they have been up to."

"Jack!"

"Hey, he brought her a present. Chill out. Anyway, do you think there is a chance he has one of those chips implanted? That a vet could read it? I mean, I know our vet has that stuff and we would have to get to him later this morning, but I don't know where else to start."

The cider wasn't doing it, so we made a pot of coffee and settled down to wait to see if the kids came up with anything. An hour and a half later they came back empty-handed. I explained our plan, and we all went down to check out the hounds, who didn't seem to even notice we were there, and we went to bed. No one slept. No one admitted it either.

By five thirty in the morning, I couldn't lie in bed any longer. I got up and started pancakes and coffee and eggs and bacon. It didn't take long for everyone to wander down to the kitchen and it didn't take long for Kaylie to let the dogs up for their share. It was Christmas after all. Healthy stuff doesn't count. Not even for dogs.

We discussed the vet plan and it seemed to be the consensus that it was too early to call him; he might not be available, and so we should do something else. It was Jeremy who said, "Hey, what happens when all the vets are closed and the police catch a stray? Don't tell me they keep it in a jail cell, and not all of them have access to shelters. Do you think the local cops have a chip scanner?"

Brilliant. And the cop shop is always open. We left right then.

After some theatrics from the dog about getting in the car and out and into the police station, he was scanned. He was Bernard from Ohio and belonged to John Tailor. We got the name and address and called as soon as we got back.

…RRRRRinnnng……..RRRRRR.nnnnnnnnng

"Hello? John? John Tailor?"

"Yes, what is it."

John was not thrilled to hear from a stranger so early on Christmas day.

"I'm sorry to bother you, but we think we have your dachshund, we had him scanned and"

"*WHAT?!*"

"Your dog, he's Bernard, right? A standard short hair?"

"*My God*, wait….uh. Are you sure? I mean, we thought he was gone! He disappeared while he was with us while we were visiting my folks and, well, are you *sure?*"

"Yeah, I think so. I had the cops scan his chip. Your name came up. Seems he's been living in my basement and I didn't know it."

"I… I… hold on a second, Marge!! Marge!! Come here! They found Bernard!"

Well, now, the rest is history and you can imagine. The Tailors left straight off from home on Christmas morning, drove through the night and arrived at our place on the twenty-sixth of December.

The reunion was something. I never asked, but I think the Tailor Christmas presents remained wrapped under their tree until they got back with Bernard.

For now, Belle looks out the front window even more diligently than ever and continues to sniff around the laundry room. So far, I have not had the heart to get her a pork chop.

Maybe next Christmas morning.

BERNARD VISITS BELLE

A story in which the families of the two dogs gather after the rescue of Bernard.

JOHN AND MARGE TAILOR had been in touch with us by phone and letters and e-mail over the months since we had discovered their dachshund, Bernard, in our basement. The Tailors had lost Bernard while visiting relatives. We found him late on Christmas Eve and gave them the news on Christmas Day. Fortunately, the computer chip implanted between Bernard's shoulders had given us the information we needed to find his owners.

Then Christmas time was upon us once again and the memory of the rescue of Bernard the dachshund came to the forefront of our minds and an invitation was made by phone to the Tailors.

Rrrrrrrinnng Rrrrrrrrrring "Hello?"

"John, it's Jack, how are you doing?"

"Oh, yeah, Hi! Fine. What's up?"

I made our offer. Jill and I had thought about it for a long time. Sometimes, the relationships developed in high-stress times fade. But we thought that this one with the Tailors would hold. After all, this was over *dachshunds* for Pete's sake! We wanted to see the Tailor's again because we thought this was, well, a thing we should continue. And besides, we knew that Belle wanted to see Bernard. Well.

"Jill and I were just thinking and we wondered if you might like to make the trip up to see us here. You could bring Bernard and the two dachs could have a reunion of sorts."

John replied, "Gee, that's a great idea. But after you rescued Bernard, the deal should really be on us, not you. That is really generous of you, we would love to. But…"

"Oh, I don't mean now, the holiday season is a mess, I was thinking of after Christmas. We could spend a day or two, do dinner and all of that while the dogs did their thing."

John said, "Boy, that sounds good, I have some time off from work after the New Year and we could drive up again, that is, if Marge agrees."

I said, "tell Marge it's a done deal, you guys pick the date, ok?"

"Great… it sounds great," replied John. "But let me wait until I talk to Marge and I need to fix us up with a motel room."

"Wrong answer, John, you guys stay with us, all right?"

"Okay. I'll talk to Marge. You sure we can bring Bernard?"

"That's the whole point!"

A couple of phone calls later, all of the arrangements had been made. Bernard was on his way to see our Belle.

Little did we know what would transpire.

Ahem.

Bernard, Marge and John showed up on our doorstep in mid January at about six in the evening. The doorbell rang, Belle started her customary barking and growling and we answered the door. Bernard was in Marge's arms and he immediately went airborne, leaped down to the floor and the two dogs began to bark, bare teeth, raise hackles, wag tails and sniff at each other. Privately I thought, *boy, I couldn't do all that at one time… these dogs must have a different set of nerve endings than me!* And they were FAST!

Marge said, "Oh goodness!"

I said, "Don't give a worry, the dogs will be fine, come in here already!" *God,* I thought, *what did I just say?* "give a worry?" My

Jamaican accent must be loose. Or was that Australian? Oh well. Not to mind, bother, no problem, whatever.

The two dogs, Belle and Bernard, proceeded to race around the living room, up and down the stairs to the family room and bedrooms and continued to bark, snarl and wag tails before we even had a chance to greet the Tailor's. *Shoot, and darn it anyway*, I thought, *let the dogs go, it's THEIR reunion after all.*

Stepping into the house John said, "Hey, thanks for having us, great to see you guys again." Marge, who looked at the dogs (who had now made the circuit of the house and returned to living room) followed him in and then she said, "Oh, yes, thank you. My goodness!"

Jill took their suitcases to the guestroom and I took their coats. Marge wore a cloth coat with a fake fur collar and John had on a quilted vest. At that point, as I was hanging the coats, Jill came down after putting the suitcases away (they were just overnight bags). Marge was still clutching a black vinyl purse, the kind that you hang over the arm. The kind you see ladies carry to church on Sunday. She wore a pair of those black pumps with the squarish heels. She was *not* going to let go of that purse.

As the dog's scruffled around in the background, I looked at Marge. Under the coat, she had on a sort of "old lady's" dress: printed rayon, princess collar and a belted waist. I was tempted to look around to see if her hose had lines up the back. John was wearing a shirt and pair of pants that looked like something straight out of LL Bean.

Hmm.

We felt under-dressed. I had on a sweatshirt and my favorite jeans with the holes in all the goofy places and Jill had on her special bib overalls with a rag sweater underneath. I thought Jill looked great and the overalls had lots of pockets for dog treats and stuff. But I sensed that Marge thought we looked like a couple of Jack Pine savages not fit for company in a civilized society.

Oh boy.

Jill gave me a look that said that maybe we should have been better dressed for our guests. I had a giggly thought in my head that, well, the dogs were naked anyway, so let's not set a higher standard. Even so, I was thinking and Jill told me later that she agreed with me that Marge was dressed a little schoolmarmish. Actually, she looked a little weird. And she was a real contrast to John. I guess in all of the excitement when they had traveled up to collect their lost dachs last winter, we had not really looked at them in detail. Now we did.

Hmmm.

Ahem. (I've always kept telling myself to buy a pipe. This would have been an excellent time to pause and light one.)

I did not have a lot of time to "hmmm" to myself. The dogs were back at it.

They raced all over. They stopped in the living room, went nose to nose in full snarly mode, and pawed at each other with a vengeance. Then they took off again like the two little carpet rockets they were designed to be.

"Go to it, guys!" I said. "Enjoy yourselves!" The dogs could be heard in the other rooms. They were having a good old time. You could hear them scrabbling over the carpet and woofing and barking and snorting.

"My goodness!" said Marge.

Yes, indeed.

I had no idea how to break the ice. I should have bought that pipe!

"John, Marge," I said, "Come on in the kitchen and we can pour a drink or two. Then we can plan the evening. What can I get you? Wine, beer? I've got stuff to make some mixes, the usually brown and white bottles and…"

John replied quickly, "uh, Marge doesn't drink, but I'd be glad for a beer to…"

Marge interrupted, "My Goodness, John, don't you think it is a little early? I'll take a white soda, by the way if you have one."

Oh, boy. This could be trouble. And I looked out the window. Early? It was already dark out for heaven's sake. What was going on here?

On the other hand, Marge had finally managed to string more than four words together in one breath. That was a hopeful sign.

I locked eyes with Jill, who was giving me no help at all and the dachshunds continued to wreak havoc with the carpet in the next room. I ploughed ahead as I tend to do, "Ok, a beer, a soda, Jill? White wine?" (She nodded silently, eyebrows up.)

"Coming straight away." I made the drinks and poured myself two fingers of scotch. I figured I would need it over time if I sipped it. The dogs could be heard still doing reconstructive surgery on the carpet in the next room. As I tended to things over the sink, I didn't hear even a whisper of conversation from the three adults behind me. All I could hear was the dogs.

Not good.

But we did our best for our guests.

Steaks went on the grill, potatoes went in the oven and the veggies went into the microwave. Salads were put together after much chopping and dinner was served.

Marge sort of stared at her plate.

"Marge," I asked. "Is your steak too rare or too well done? I can put it back on if it's too rare. Or I could nuke it…"

John replied for Marge. "Marge doesn't eat meat"

Oh. I wish I had known. "I guess the dogs will be having a treat, then, hey?"

No response from Marge. But she nibbled at potatoes, salad and veggies.

The rest of the evening didn't go much better. Getting a response out of Marge was a real challenge and John tried his best to sort of look past her attitude as though he was embarrassed. He told a few jokes. I told a few back. But Marge just never seemed to warm up to the situation. Jill tapped her foot a lot and put a good dent in the wine supply.

Finally, we decided to retire to bed and agreed to make plans for the next day in the morning. Belle and Bernard were taken out to the back yard and after much encouragement did their thing. Jill and I rewarded the two dogs with cookies from Belle's supply. Bed was in order. Jill and I retired to our room and the Tailors went to our guestroom with Bernard.

All seemed quiet, if not a little tense. I really thought once again about a pipe. I could have stoked it up by the fireplace and just sort of sat and thought about everything in a dignified manner. But I just turned in.

It must have been about two in the morning of the next day when there was a knock on our bedroom door. It was Marge.

I opened the door, bleary eyed and a little headachy from the scotch, to see Marge standing in the hall in a flannel set of pajamas covered by a flannel robe with our Belle under one arm. I could not help but stare, blurred vision and all, at the robe Marge was wearing. It was printed all over with little phrases. Some said "Warm

Toes—Warm Heart!" Others said "Home Is Where the Heart Is!" They were printed all over at odd angles.

"Excuse me," she said to me, "but *your* dog has snuck into our room and has been getting our Bernard way too excited. I *hope* I don't have to be specific. Would you please take her back?"

I did, of course. And then I conjured up the best sheepish grin I could give. It did not seem to have an effect. Oh, well. I was not thinking that I was being all that effectual lately anyway.

Pipe, I thought, *if I just had a pipe!*

I inserted Belle back under the covers of our bed and thought, Marge *does* talk. Hmm. I seemed to be hmming a lot. Jill rolled over, propped up on one arm and said, "grmph?"

I said, "Never mind, it isn't worth it. Go back to sleep."

"Okramph," she said.

I did go right back to sleep but I dreamed of dachshunds carrying miniature black vinyl purses in their little jaws.

In the morning, once every one was up and getting the sleep out of their eyes, we planned for Jill and Marge to do some shopping. John and I would tour some of my computer network installations. The men would find lunch separate from the women somewhere. Then we would have dinner back at the house. With some discreet inquiry, we discovered Marge would eat fish or chicken. Boiled or broiled, please, nothing rich.

We got through breakfast fine with one exception.

A chunk of butter-and-syrup-soaked pancake from one of our plates hit the floor. Bernard came racing into the room at the sound of the wet plop and stopped and stood over the messy fragment. He began to growl and snarl, his lips were drawn way back from his teeth and his ears were flat against the side of his head.

"Bernard! Stop it," exclaimed John.

"My goodness!" (You *know* who said that, right?)

I reached down to Bernard with one hand to perhaps calm him only to have him snap at me. I then knew what writers talk about in horror stories about the click of the monster's teeth on air. It was a *loud* click and it startled me.

"*Hey!*" I said in surprise. (I am not eloquent when startled) Bernard continued to bristle and snarl over the piece of pancake. I was thinking that maybe I should get a paper towel. And maybe some heavy leather gloves.

As the humans sat stunned at the table and as Bernard continued to play up a miniature version of a tyrannosaurus Rex, Belle sort of wandered in. Her movement through the kitchen was slow and she paid little attention to anyone. She ambled over to the pancake particle and Bernard. We all sat transfixed for a moment.

"Belle! *No!*" (We all contributed to that one—it was sort of a chorus.)

An old song popped into my head. I think it had been recorded by the Eagles.

Somebody's gonna hurt someone, before the night is through!
Somebody's gonna come undone, there's nothing we can do!

Yet nothing happened, really. Bernard backed off, and Belle nosed down to the pancake and removed the syrup and butter off of the floor in about five licks as Bernard supervised.

Ok, I got it.

My daughter, Kaylie, during Bernard's last "visit", had tried to explain something to me when Bernard brought a pork chop scrap to Belle when he had been lost and then found in our basement the previous Christmas. She'd insisted that Bernard had brought Belle a present. I scoffed at that offering, but Kaylie insisted that Bernard had brought that scrap of pork as a present for Belle. Kaylie had been right. Bernard had a special spot in his little heart for our Belle. The pancake event must have been just a different manifestation of the behavior Kaylie had observed at Christmas.

Amazing.

Sort of cute, too.

I looked across the table and caught Jill's eye. Without looking away from Jill, I said, "Well, now. Bernard seems to continue to be the real gentleman. First it has been gifts of pork and now pancakes. He is quite the little guy, hey?"

Belle snorted and Bernard gave out a soft "wuff."

"Pork chops?" asked John. "What are you talking about?"

"My goodness," stated Marge.

Marge was *really* beginning to wear on me. But…

I explained about the pork chop. When we had finally found the lost Bernard in our basement last Christmas, he had a scrap of pork chop with a bit of green ribbon stuck to it with him. He let Belle eat the thing. Daughter Kaylie had said that Bernard had brought it as a present for Belle and I had said he just had dug it out of the garbage for himself and someone's trashed Christmas wrap had stuck to it. I was wrong, clearly. So I was told.

"So," I finished, "the pancake is the same sort of thing. You see? It's another present!"

Marge and John did not see at all. In fact, they looked at me as though I had a toad growing out of the middle of my forehead. Jill rescued me, "Jack, come help me clean up the dishes while John and Marge go up stairs and get ready. We are going out, still?"

Yeah, dishes, I thought to myself. *That would be good.* The toad and I went to help clean up. Of course the dachshunds had to help, licking and slurping the remains of breakfast off of the plates. Hey, you wouldn't believe what we save in dishwasher soap at our house.

As we two men were about to leave the house in my Blazer and the two women were about to leave in Jill's car, I took Jill aside. "Are you going to be all right with Marge? I mean, she seems a little…"

Jill blew me off. "Forget it, I have plans. You'll see. Just you and John go and have a good time. Play with your 'puters and show John around some of the places around the lake. I have it under control. Okay?"

"Uh, yeah. Okay." I had doubts. But I also knew Jill. Actually, that's what scared me a little. What did she have in mind?

"See you?" I said cautiously.

"Ok, see you guys! Jill said, "Have fun. We will! C'mon, Marge. Let these two fools to themselves. You and I are going shopping." And then having said that, Jill bustled Marge out of the house, into Jill's car, and they were down the driveway before I could say another thing at all.

John looked at me with his eyebrows up and his head lowered, pressing his chin down against his chest.

I shrugged. "Let's make sure the dogs are set before we go, John. I don't know exactly when we'll be back and who knows when the ladies will be back. You fill the water dishes and I'll put some chow out. We'll have to get the two of them out for their business. You take Bernard out front and I'll take Belle in the back. They won't waste time dinking around with each other that way."

John and I climbed into my Blazer after we tended to the dogs and we were on our way. I had a thought, as we drove off, that the ladies could, well, get into some kind of trouble. But I really couldn't get that thought to coalesce. Something ticked and ticked in the back of my head that something or other was about to transpire.

"Say, Jack? Where are we going?"

"Huh? I mumbled.

John had been talking while I was ruminating. He repeated himself, "Where are we going?"

"John, I am going to show you some of my network installations in some of the buildings that I have been working in if you are interested. After that, we're going to stop at a place I know. You will like it. It's the *Golden Wolf* over on the end of Pensive Lake. We'll get a good sandwich and beer or two there. Ok with you?"

"Great, that sounds great. But I have to ask you a question."

"Sure, I said. "Shoot."

"You know, I love my wife." John sounded guilty.

"Uh, yeah? Hey, guy, how about Bernard" I thought where was *this* going?

John struggled with the next, "Sometimes she..."

John must've missed my point of humor about Bernard.

"Stop it John, not a problem. Do you think we should skip the computer tour and hit the *Golden Wolf?*"

John adjusted his frame, sat visibly straighter in his seat and said, "You know? If that's okay with you it sounds great to me. I really don't know much about computers anyway. They gave me one at work, but I don't really know much about them anyway. Let's just go."

"Great! They've got great burgers at the *Golden Wolf* and we can have a couple of beers while the wives are out spending our money."

John said ruefully, "Ain't that the truth! 'Course you know, Marge doesn't really spend that much. Not on clothes or stuff like that."

I bit my tongue.

John had one more thing, "Do you think the dogs will be all right?"

"Yeah, sure. Don't worry. We won't stay long."

The *Golden Wolf* was full of the usual Saturday crowd; lake people that couldn't sail or get their power boats out during the winter and were looking for something to do. It was a polite group. Two or three people were at the bar sipping whatever and a half dozen pairs were at tables in the atrium overlooking Pensive Lake. I motioned John to a table and we sat. A waitress, Shannon, one that I knew, approached.

"Hi, Jack!" she said. "Who's this?" The waitress cast one of those sunrise smiles at John. (I thought, maybe I should just tell her he was married right off and be on with things, but I didn't'—I guess I thought that was John's call, not mine.)

"Hello, yourself," I posted back, "this is John. He has a dachshund, just like me."

"John, hello. Nice to meet you! Did Jack here ever tell you about the story about Bernard? It is so *cute*! I could just *die*!"

Shannon smiled again. And I thought that maybe I should be wearing my sunglasses. That, or maybe with all of those teeth in view from that smile, I might maybe call a dentist. Or maybe an orthodontist.

I told her. "This is *the* John, Shannon. He's the one who owns Bernard. He and his wife Marge are the ones in the story. They're visiting and we are here to grab a sandwich."

"*No!* You're kidding! John!? Are you the one with the, the dachshund dog who took a pork chop present to Jack's Belle? We all know Belle. She's a sweetheart, really. She's been in here! And we sneak her little treats and stuff. Oh, I shouldn't have said that.

We don't allow dogs in here, but Belle is different and she always is *so* good and, *gosh* I don't believe it!"

I laughed. "Yeah, this is John, famous owner of Bernard, right here on this very stage. And by the way, Belle and Bernard are back at the house so we need to get going here. Can you get us two mushroom and Swiss burgers, fries and a couple of light beers? Mugs?"

"You bet. That'll be right up. Bernard! I can't *believe* it!"

I looked over the table at John. He was sitting straight up, his hands were down in his lap and his eyes were casting back and forth between the view of the frozen surface of Pensive Lake and the inside of the *Golden Wolf*. For just a second, just a micro second, I thought that I was seeing Marge, not John.

No, I said to myself. *This can't be.* I was confused.

"John!"

"Hmmph?"

I told him to relax. I told him that Marge and Jill were off having a great time and that Shannon was an innocent dear and that the burgers that were coming were going to be the very best he ever had.

We inhaled the burgers. We chewed and swallowed the French fries that we had slopped with ketchup. I wrapped a piece of burger in a napkin for Belle. John did the same for Bernard. We slurped down two beers each and then headed home to the dogs.

I wondered if the women had returned before the two of us guys. Somehow, I doubted that.

After arriving back at the house, we put the dogs out, watered them and then put out the scraps of hamburger we had brought back. Staying in style, Bernard stood over his scrap of hamburger until Belle finished hers. Belle snapped up Bernard's treat as he watched. (I put the extra hamburger that Shannon had snuck into my coat pocket, encased in one of those Styrofoam things, in the fridge. I figured it would make a great late night snack for me and the dogs.)

I told John to have a seat in the living room. I grabbed the remote and thumbed on a sports channel. As we watched men in expensive clothing catch fish neither of us had ever even dreamed of, Belle clambered into my lap and Bernard crawled into John's.

Perfect day.

So far.

Somewhere around fifteen fish later, the doorbell rang. Of course the two dachshunds went into doozle diddy fits. They jumped from our lazy laps, hit the floor running and attacked the front door. I had a thought that, gee, I would never match the paint needed to repair the claw marks.

Oh, well.

The two of them were barking, snarling and jumping. The two of them looked like two elongated brown popcorn kernels bouncing up from the bottom of a stove top pan.

I got up and opened the front door. Two women were standing there. One was Jill. I didn't recognize the other one.

The dachshunds were still snarling and barking and bouncing around like two unstriped matching Tiggers from *Winnie the Pooh*. John joined me at the door and was immediately foot tangled with the two dogs.

Jill said, "Hey, grab the dogs, are you going to let us in or not?"

Us?

As Jill and the other gal came into the house, stepping around the dogs, I took a good long look at the person who was not my wife.

She was a knockout. Drop dead beautiful. She wore white, skintight stretch pants and a blue semi-transparent blouse that showed off a body that could cause accidents. Her hair and makeup looked like something out of a fashion magazine; *Cosmo*, maybe.

Whew!

"What do you think?" Jill said. "We gave Marge a change. We picked out some new clothes and did one of those makeover places at the mall." Jill stood grinning.

Ok, this second lady was Marge. I was dumbfounded. I *knew* Jill would have been up to something, but boy...

"What do you think, John?" Jill asked. "Isn't she great?!"

Marge did a slow turn for John. I was glad I didn't miss it. John was darn near speechless, but he said:

"Oh my goodness!"

Jill really had done a number on Marge. The clothes. The makeup. It was unbelievable. John could not take his eyes off of her. Jill couldn't stop grinning. Bernard was barking a holy fit. He did not recognize this stranger at all. I didn't see Belle, then. I suspected she had gone upstairs to hide in her favorite closet.

I thought about joining her.

Marge, amazingly, had a little smile on her face. I guess Jill really had made a change. Inside and out.

I felt I had to say something to break the moment. "Ok, Guys. Boy, Marge. You look great! Um, let me go start dinner. I was thinking of marinated grilled chicken?

Marge was the one who answered. "That sounds scrumptious. Don't you think, John?"

John didn't answer, he just kept staring. He was completely nonplussed.

Marge? I thought. I couldn't quite accept the change. She *talked!* I wanted to look over my shoulder to see if Rod Serling was around somewhere. Bernard continued to fit and bark and carry on.

I thought, hey, I'm with you, Bernard. Pretty Cool.

Jill kicked me, gently, in the ankle. She moved her lips, wordlessly, saying "Easy, Jack, remember me?"

Right. Bernard continued to bark and shuffle and I went to start dinner.

Marge had made an amazing transformation. Not only did she look like she would stop traffic; she actually participated in our conversations. She didn't say a lot, but she was not as silent and as reserved, as she had been when she first arrived.

At one point she said, "Tell me, Jack, did that story you told about the pork chop really happen? It's so hard to believe. But after seeing Bernard and the pancake this morning, I can't help but want to think it's true."

I answered her, talking around a mouthful of chicken. "Yup, it happened. Just like I said this morning. But it wasn't me who figured the whole thing out; it was my daughter, Kaylie who saw the truth of things. Your Bernard must really have a soft spot in his little heart for our Belle."

During this exchange, we all could hear the dogs whining and scruffling and snorting in the next room. None of the four of us gave it a thought. The dogs had been running around the household for two days now and the sounds they had been making had become "white noise." So, we paid no attention.

John saw fit to compliment my marinated chicken.

Jill sipped her wine.

The dogs continued to wuff and snort in the next room.

As I sat at the table, my back was to the living room. Marge sat across from me so that if she chose to look, she would be able to see the room behind me in which the dogs were playing.

Suddenly, Marge turned bone white. "*Oh my God!*" Her eyes were riveted on a spot over my shoulder in the next room where the dogs were... playing.

"*Oh my God!*" Marge said again. I figured I should turn around and look at what was getting her so excited. I did.

It was Belle and Bernard that had captured Marge's attention. They had been making those snuffling and whining noises while we humans were eating dinner. Belle and Bernard, were, well...

Doing it.

Oh boy.

John jumped from his seat, knocking his chair backward in his rush to get to his dog. "Bernard! *No!*"

Too late. The two hounds separated. Belle took off for the upstairs rooms; a blurry, furry brown rocket streaking over up the carpeted stairs. Bernard stood a moment and then slumped over on his side. He appeared a little breathless.

I couldn't help it. I never can. I blurted out, "Hey, someone get Bernard a cigarette!"

No one was amused. Oh well.

John started to apologize. Marge was visibly shaken. Jill and I looked at each other....what was there to say?

Marge said in a shaken voice, "Jill, do you still have some of that white wine?"

The rest of that evening, considering what had gone on, went well. Marge's new image plus a couple of glasses of Chablis went a long way to make her feel comfortable and to open up and laugh at this or that. I caught her blinking her lashes at John on a couple of occasions. Eventually, Belle came trucking down the stairs from where she had secreted herself after the Bernard event. She put her front paws on Marge's leg and Marge pulled her up off the floor into her lap.

"What a sweetheart!" said Marge.

"That's what Shannon said," said John. I think he immediately regretted it.

"Shannon?" asked Marge.

John blustered, "Oh, Shannon, she's a waitress at the *Golden Wolf* and Jack introduced us and she knows Belle and…"

"Oh, John. Shut up, you silly." Marge didn't seem to have a care other than to hold Belle and pet her. Then she surprised us all.

"John, let's go to bed early. Jack and Jill, do you mind?"

We didn't. Both dogs snoozed in our bed that night.

Marge and John slept in the next morning. I can only guess why. I took care of feeding and watering and getting the dogs outside. Once up and awake, Marge surprised me one more time by coming to breakfast in a duplicate outfit of Jill's. She had purchased a set of bib overalls and a rag sweater, just like Jill's. She wore the outfit proudly.

I snuck a chunk of scrambled eggs to Bernard, knowing he would deliver it to Belle.

John spent a lot of time grinning that morning.

Marge and John packed, collected Bernard and prepared to leave for their trip back. Lots had changed, thanks to Jill and, maybe, the dogs. John was still grinning. Marge gave me a kiss on the cheek that lasted a split second longer than I thought it should. Maybe I just imagined it. But John looked on proudly and Jill had a smile on her face that was surely stolen from an elf.

Cradled in Marge's arms, Bernard looked sadly over her shoulder as his owners headed down the drive to their car. *Belle?* He seemed to say. *When can I see you again?*

Ahem, sorry, maybe that was a bit of a reach. But you get the idea.

As the Tailors backed their car down the drive and headed off, disappearing at the end of the street, Jill and I waved from the front door. Belle barked.

There was one thought left in my head after all of this; just one word, actually, and the word was not "pipe" it was—

Puppies.

The Mouse
That Was Saved

The Story of the Puppies of Belle and Bernard, the Adventures of a Field Mouse, the Intervention of Luck and the Application of Things That Are Good and Kind.

I BROKE MY ARM ONCE. It was bad. My bones were sticking out of my skin and I could see them. Once, I had stitches sewn in my mouth after I fell on my face and pushed my top teeth all the way through my lower lip. I witnessed, and aided, hands-on, the birth of both of my children. I never faltered during any of these events.

But when Belle was delivering her first puppy, I fainted. I really did. And I smacked my forehead on the floor after going down and then faded away on the ceramic floor tiles in the kitchen. I fell just inches away from the birthing box we had set there for our pregnant dachshund. Jill got the vet on the on the phone, listened to Dr. Aspin's advice and took care of things while I was passed out.

After the visit of the dachshund, Bernard and our friends Marge and John, Belle had become "with puppies." And while we looked forward to the birth of these palm-sized little critters, I missed most of it. By the time I woke up (Jill just left me there on the floor, threw a blanket over me and figured I would wake up on my own), it was time to call the Tailors and tell them about the arrival of the four puppies—three boys and a girl. They were thrilled when I called and told them that the mating between our Belle and their Bernard had finally resulted in the birth of the little pups.

Over the phone, one on each extension, both of them said, "My goodness!" It was a duet, nothing new. These folks, owners of our Belle's sire, were not always that eloquent. They were uncomplicated people. That is a different story. Read the last one. We promised to arrange a visit in the future to have the Tailors see the pups.

Belle and the puppers thrived. Belle nursed them, nosed them around as a dachshund mom should in terms of discipline and eventually, as they grew a little older and bolder and bigger, she nosed them out of the dog bed and into the real world.

The world of the kitchen, that is.

Jill and I could not help but giggle and chuckle at the pups' antics. They had nearly no control of their legs, and their little noses looked nothing like the noses of their adult peers. Their noses were so short! And it was all they could do to even get upright on the kitchen tiles. Eventually they did manage it. And then they became horrors. They were *everywhere*.

Once they found their voices, it was auditory bedlam.

An example: one afternoon I came home from work and I was looking forward to doing a little more work in my office on the lower floor of our home.

Not.

Jill greeted me at the door. Actually, greeted is the wrong word. She pounced on me. "Jack, *do* something with these *puppies!*"

I could hear them; "*Whine*", slobber, "*Whine! Rife, Rife, Riife, Riffe, RIIFFE!*" The sounds sort of really did hurt one's ears.

The four of them produced such a cacophony of puppy dog noises that I could not hear Jill's "greeting." The little dogs were galloping and darting around the enclosed kitchen like mad lizards.

"Huh?"

"Jack!"

"What was that? I can't hear you, Jill, the pups are too loud."

I was in immediate trouble. I could tell this. I'd had lots of experience.

This is what I sort of heard. I am interpreting but it's pretty close.

"I've been with these *bark* dogs all day *woof, snarl* and *yipe* you don't do a thing, and I have *yipe yipe yipe* just about had it *yip yipe* and you come home *yipe yipe* and just don't do anything and these dogs are driving me nuts and… and *woof* if you think you are going to…"

It was hard to tell which came from Jill and which came from the dogs, but, I was grateful when she ran out of breath. Jill that is. I thought so, anyway. Had I actually heard her bark? Never mind, I wasn't going there.

The pups did not, however, become breathless and their mom, Belle, joined into the fray.

Communication was out of the question. So I did what all good dog owners do in times of crises. I got food. I went to the cupboard, grabbed some dog cookies, really little ones, and threw them on the kitchen floor.

Save for the sounds of scrambling claws and paws on tiles and the crunching of sharp little teeth, miniature carnivores breaking the bones of their prey, all was quiet for a moment or two.

"Now, Jill, you were saying?"

Too late. Jill whirled and left the room. I can't say I blamed her. I was the one, now, surrounded by pups looking for their next whatever. Belle looked up at me (I never have understood how those little dachshunds can bend their necks up so far to look at you from the floor) as if to say:

"Well, big guy? Now what?"

What indeed? And the pups, having finished their wolf bait, began to howl and yip and bark once more.

Life went on like that for a while.

Things *did* settle down. The little pups' noses grew and Belle was a good mom; nursing till it was time to stop and cooperating with the weaning. Suddenly, out of the blue, we noticed that we had five real dachshunds in the house. How did that happen? I spent more time scooping poop than I did writing or working at anything else. As cute as the little things were, it was becoming a real chore to take care of all of the feeding and cleaning and cuddling and such.

One night, Belle came up to our bedroom to take her usual place at the bottom of the bed, to be ensconced under the covers, breathing down there with a method known only to dachshunds… we have certainly never figured it out. How do they breathe like that? This time all four pups were in tow.

And up they came. Belle insisted, and we lifted each one up and each in turn found a place to burrow. Actually, there was lots of room. But the leftover space was good for only one adult human. Jill and I began each taking turns sleeping on one of the downstairs couches.

Things progressed in reasonable fashion with the puppies. We made some adjustments. The major one was that we bought a bigger bed.

The little dogs' noses elongated and they became actual dachshunds, recognizable by most anyone. This did not always include those that would see us on the street walking with five dogs. These folks would ask what kind of dogs the puppies were. We always responded that they were baby Dobermans. That usually quelled any further irritating questions. It was amazing. People would reach down to pet our crowd of pups and then snatch their hands back, (after we told them the dogs' heritage) smiling and saying, "Oh, really?" Our household has always been haunted with a strange sense of humor. It could be from the paint on the walls or something. Don't really know.

Fall came to our part of the world. Leaves colored themselves, then browned, fell and made a mess in the yard. These are pretty at first, but a real problem. And when a household has five dachshunds, the residents can become crazed trying to keep track of the dogs in the leaves. It seems the color of most dachshunds blends in just perfectly with fallen leaves. Fall has its problems.

And there are mice in fall.

Anyone who has ever lived in a four-season climate knows that the local little rodents want to invade and establish residence inside warm human habitations for the winter as fall begins. In our case, we had been through this migration for so many seasons that we were (we thought) veterans of prevention. We had always taken the usual precautions.

Belle did not think so. She began to edge.

The word "Edge" has a special definition at our house. It is a verb, actually, used in common speech as "edging." As in, "there goes Belle, she's edging!" The little dachshund began to spend lots of time covering all of the corners of the basement office and laundry room. She would stick her nose into the joints formed by the wall and floor and then travel all along the perimeter of the rooms, snuffling and snorting and (we presumed) looking for rodents.

There weren't any. We were sure of this. All of the mouse egresses had been filled, caulked, wired over and stopped up. We were mouse professionals.

But Belle continued to edge. And soon the pups joined in. This was driving us crazy. Every morning, every afternoon, every *hour* the dogs begged to go downstairs and sniff for mice. If the door wasn't open, they would sit and whine at the top of the stairs. If we were sleeping, they would bark and yip until we let them down there in the lower office and basement laundry room.

"Hey, guys! *There are no mice!"*

Yeah, right, like they would all listen to me. Good luck.

By now, in the season of the mouse hunt, the pups had names; Roller, Prancer, Snort and Lampshake. The names speak for themselves and need no explanation. That is except for Lampshake. This one was named because this pup spent most of his time running around the house like a wildcat in pursuit of dinner. In most cases, he would ram into table legs and topple the lamps on those tables. Hence; Lampshake.

I did relent on the mouse thing. I finally gave in and told the dogs that while I *really* did not think there was a mouse down below, I would set one of the live traps, just in case. I didn't think it necessary, mind you, but maybe this might keep some peace. I would show the dogs that there were no mouses once and for all.

Mice, I meant, Mice. My god! I was beginning to talk like the dogs! Did I just say that? Was I thinking that the dogs could talk? I was not in good shape. Too many dogs and too few mice, I guess.

Ahem.

The next morning a mouse was in the live trap, feasting on the peanut butter I'd placed there as bait.

Roller was the first to find it. He had rumble bumped down the stairs to the trap and began to howl at about five thirty in the a.m. This howling woke up Snort. Snort heard Roller howling from his place under the bedcovers and began to, well, snort. Never moving from under the bedcovers, he was making all kinds of wet, messy, nose-based noises. Prancer joined in with grunts and woofs.

Down in the back of the basement, Roller held guard by the trap until I rose from my bed to see what the matter was. Belle followed me down to see Roller next to the trap, on his back, feet in air and teeth bared. The mouse cowered in the trap; peanut butter forgotten.

Well I'll be, I thought. *The dogs win, I lose. We have mice!*

And now it was time for an immediate disposal. I grabbed a piece of newspaper and placed the trap on it so as to catch the droppings out of the bottom of the wire mesh of the trap. I was a mouse expert, after all. Climbing up the stairs, dogs in tow, I carried the trap to the patio doors and then headed out to the woods behind the house with the trapped rodent. I had to shake the trap with doors opened to get the little thing loose. It fell out, adjusted its whiskers and scampered off under the fallen leaves. The score then, sat at Dogs—1, Mouse—1 and Jack—0.

Returning to the house I was greeted by all six; Belle, Prancer, Lampshake, Roller, Snort and Jill. It seemed like a homecoming save for the live trap I was holding under my arm. I had five dogs pawing at my legs and my wife pawing at my arm. The snorting, rolling, shaking and prancing told me I should allow the dogs to sniff the trap to make sure they knew the mouse was gone. The pawing at my arm; that was another problem. I had to explain to Jill that a mouse had breached our defenses. Oh boy.

I re-baited and reset the trap and placed it back in the basement. I had to put an upside-down orange crate over the top of it so the curious hounds would not trip the trap with their inquisitive noses.

The next morning, again at five, Roller took off out of the bed, scrambled to the basement and began to howl while lying on his back next to the orange crate. Snort leaped from the bed, trucked down the stairs and joined in with nose noises. Belle ambled down and sat nearby watching the festivities. There was another mouse in the live trap.

I took that little critter, again, out to the woods behind the house, cleaned, re-baited the trap and set it up under the orange crate once more. Now the score was Mice—2, Dogs—2 and Jack—0. The score changed, not in my favor, once more the next morning.

Roller woke us all up at five in the morning to make sure we knew we had caught the third mouse. This time Jill joined me down in the back room.

Rubbing the night's sleep from her eyes, Jill leaned down to peer into the mouse trap. "Ooo, look at him! He's so cute, I want to pet him."

I rolled my eyes. "You can't pet it; it's a mouse. It'll bite you."

"I want to pet him!" When an idea arrives in Jill's head, it is very, very difficult to knock loose.

Prancer and Lampshake arrived. All five dogs began to bristle and growl, ears back, heads thrust forward and ready to pounce. "Alright, fine," I said to my wife, "I'll see if I can get it out of the trap and you can pet the darn thing while I hold it. But then I have to take it outside, OK?" I reached for a work glove on the nearby bench, lifted the trap off of the concrete floor and placed it on the bench. I wriggled the glove onto my right hand and then, securing the trap with my left, I fingered open the door and reached in.

Of all of the mistakes I have made in my life, I will not forget that one. The mouse escaped.

The racing rodent hit the top of the workbench, stumbled on its side, righted it self and leaped to the floor. It landed right in the middle of the dachshund herd. The canine reaction was electric. I don't know how this is possible, but all five of the little hounds froze in place and began to shake at the same time.

The mouse lost no time investigating. It took off across the floor and headed for the stairs in the next room.

Did you ever see one of those runaway stage coaches on some old television western being pulled by panicked horses with the wooden wheels of the coach just blurs? That was what the little mouse legs and feet looked like: blurred stage coach wheels. Up the stairs went the mouse. The dogs broke out of their suspended state, took off after the mouse and erupted into full throttle and throat.

You would have thought a pack of wolves was after an elk in our house. It was either that or a fox hunt. I thought for a second that I would hear a hunting trumpet start to blare. In any event, the chase was on and I joined in. As I scrambled up the stairs at the tail of the scrambling herd of hounds, I thought two quick thoughts. I was going to need the carpet cleaners to remove the carnage I was sure to see and I was going to need vet Aspin to check on the hounds after mouse ingestion.

The mouse reached the first floor with the dogs right behind. The howling and growling and baying were deafening. I don't think even a hunting trumpet could have been heard above the din. Carpet fibers flew. The mouse darted one way and then, in full panic, another and the hounds tried to twist and reel and keep up. At one point, the mouse completely reversed, ran right through Snort's front legs, streaked underneath his belly and out between his back legs. Snort lowered his head and tried to look down and back between his legs as the mouse exited under his tail. The mouse headed for a corner of the room and then dead-ended, cowering against the baseboards. The dogs, still barking and howling, surrounded it. But for some reason known only to them, they did not pounce.

Rigid, with lips drawn back, the dogs stood shoulder to shoulder, forming a barrier, keeping the mouse at bay in the corner. They looked like a bunch of big furry sardines crammed in a can or maybe a bunch of carp all pointed in the same direction. I could hear growls deep in throats and I've never seen so many teeth at once. Without much thought, I ankled my way in between the hounds, reached down with my still-gloved hand and grabbed the little mouse.

"Ha!" I said.

Jill caught up to all of us just as the hunt had ended. She still wanted to pet the mouse. I just sighed and presented the little creature while held in my fist. His bewhiskered snout and tiny head with its black eyes stuck out of the ring formed by my forefinger and thumb. Jill extended an index finger and stroked the mouse's head.

"He's so soft!"

"Just don't get bit, I have to take him out back." The mouse was beginning to wriggle in my hand and the dogs had broken formation to jump and paw at my legs. I raised the mouse aloft and out of harm's way; both human and canine.

"Jack?" asked Jill, "Could this be the same mouse?"

"Huh?"

Jill continued, "What is this, three in three days? I'll bet you're catching the same mouse over and over. I mean, you just take him out to the woods and that isn't very far away so it could just be the same mouse coming back."

"No way, why would the same mouse keeping getting him self caught in the same trap? That's silly," I argued.

"Maybe it just has a thing for peanut butter," Jill suggested.

I didn't want to admit to my wife that she might be right and that it may have been futile trapping and releasing the same mouse. And all that was really going on was that the dogs were waking us when a mouse was in the trap and after this little"hunt" I was getting tired of the whole thing.

So I said, "Ok, let's experiment. C'mon back downstairs with me."

Mouse clutched in hand, dogs and Jill in tow, I descended once more and approached the bench in the back room.

"See that old bottle of model paint?" I pointed to a quarter ounce jar of Testor's enamel on a shelf. It was probably left over from a project one of our kids had worked on a while ago when they were still kids. "Open it up, would you? I can't use both hands, I don't want to let go of the mouse."

While Jill struggled with the cap and the dogs stared up and bristled, I grabbed a small brush with my free hand. Jill opened and then held the small jar out for me. The color was neon pink. Using the brush and paint, I proceeded to give the mouse a pink punker hairdo.

I thought this little trick might put the issue to rest. "Ok," I said to everyone, "if this mouse is stupid enough to come back, we'll know. We can't miss it."

Jill had a question about whether the paint might hurt the mouse but I dismissed it. However I did wonder if I was not marking the little thing as a target for the local hawks and other predators. I shook off that thought knowing I could not tolerate another indoor hunting party with a pack of wild dachshunds. The paint was the quick-dry kind, so the mouse was deposited then, pink head and all, in the back woods.

The next morning, promptly at five o'clock, Roller found a pink-headed mouse in the live trap. When I went down to see, I immediately took the whole trap, still mouse-inhabited, into the garage so as to avoid a repeat of the previous day's festivities. Jill joined me for coffee in the kitchen. I told her about the pink-headed mouse.

"I told you," she said.

I was waiting for that and said, "Yeah, I'm going to have to take it out far away somewhere where it can't find its way back. I was thinking of Korsi's farm down the road."

Jill cautioned me, "I don't know if the Korsi folks would be too happy with you just dropping off some little mouse without asking about it. Can you call them?"

"Nah," I said. "What's one little mouse? Farms are full of mice."

Jill was not convinced of my plan. "What about the barn cats? They'll get the little thing!"

"Look," I said, "We can have a wild herd of dachshunds hunting in our living room while we run out of peanut butter, or the mouse can go and fend for itself. I'll put it in one of the sheds at the farm, ok?"

I knew what coming after that.

"Can I pet it before you go?"

I thought about that for a moment and started to phrase a couple different replies, but I took the conservative way out and just said,

"No."

I left the kitchen and went to the garage to place the mouse, still in the trap, into the back of my Blazer. The two of us drove out and headed down the mile to the farm. I pulled over, removed mouse and trap and headed through a field to an old utility shed. The door was latched but not locked, and I stepped in, trap under my arm.

The place smelled rusty and dusty and was full of farm tools, old bags the print on which had faded away, and a lawn tractor in the corner that listed on mostly flat tires. A couple of old canvas tarps rotted in the corner. It looked like a regular high class mouse resort in my view. I held the trap up to eye level.

"Ok, little punk rocker. Here's your stop. Hope you like it. There should be some new friends here and I think it will be a lot quieter." (Here I was going again, talking to animals!)

The mouse didn't say anything but through the wire of the trap I could see him using his back foot to scratch the top of his pink head. I said to him, "Don't worry, that stuff will wear off." I put the trap on the floor and opened it. The mouse didn't leave the trap.

I figured the little guy would vacate his prison eventually, so I left the trap in the middle of the floor and took a few steps away to inspect the stuff stored in the shed. There were scythes and rakes and shovels of all shapes and sizes. There was even a bushel of old dried corn against one wall. It was all of only mild interest until I toed over one of the tarps and what looked to be nearly twenty mice began scooting for new cover. They were everywhere.

"This is good," I thought. "Lots of mice must mean this is a good place." I turned to the trap to see that it was now empty. Okay, mission accomplished. I headed for the door.

At the door, my hand on the latch, I paused, thinking for just a second. I felt I had to say something so I turned back and called into the shed. "Hey. All you mice in here! Make this new guy feel at home! And don't be put off by that pink head. Just figure he might be from London."

THE REAL
CHRISTMAS STORY

(or, What Happened to the Gold, Frankincense and Myrrh)

THE MOON ROSE in the eastern desert sky to illuminate three resting camels and three supine human figures sleeping on the ground nearby. A fire had died to embers. The three figures stirred and then rose and stretched in the moonlight. Their coverings fell down to the ground as they rose and the rich fabrics glittered on the edges where gold and silver threads had been woven into the cloth.

These three men were kings, travelers in search of something important. A bright star in the sky at night had guided them for some time to their ultimate destination. One man spoke to the other two.

"Akim, Jelode, I can still see the star. The sun has gone to earth and we must continue."

The others answered, "Yes, I see it. We must go." and "I see it as well, Rahjem, I shall go and kick the camels, stubborn beasts as they are."

The three men packed their things, clambered up unto wooden saddles on the camels and continued their journey east under the evening sky. Each had a special package tied to his saddle.

A two hour's march away, a man and women woke to the same moon and same star. As they were poor, a single donkey would carry the woman. The man and the three dogs that traveled with them would walk. The woman, seated on a rough blanket on the back of the donkey would allow the dogs, one at a time, to rest, draped in front of her over the back of the pack animal.

The man, Joe, silently wondered why the dogs should get such treatment. He felt that the woman's willingness to share her ride might compromise the donkey's endurance. After all, the woman was pregnant, very, and he thought the dogs should have been walking along on their own.

Joe was a carpenter. And he often received payment for his work with food or clothes or other things than coin. The three dogs had been such a payment. They were small, short haired and built long and close to the ground with short legs. Rumors held they had been bred centuries ago by the Egyptian Pharaohs. Other thoughts belied this and claimed their breed came from the north. No one knew. Centuries later, a country called Germane would take credit for what would be called the "badger hounds", "dachshunds", or "teckels", in the language of the people of the region. For the moment, out on that desert, the dogs just ambled along, jumping up and nipping at the donkey's legs for a chance to ride. Joe just trudged. The woman clasped hard with her knees to side of the wobbling donkey and prayed her time would not come while out in the wilderness.

Hours later, Joe and the woman and the three hounds came upon a small village. The woman's time was very close and Joe begged shelter in a barn for the night. The dogs burrowed down in straw and hay kept there in the little structure to absorb the excretions of the pigs, goats, sheep and unseen little animals that shared the shelter. The woman lay back on the same carpet of straw and waited. Joe fidgeted and the dogs slept.

Akim, Jelode and Rahjem were only miles away. The camels plodded and the three riders were sweating into the cloths wrapped around their heads in spite of the cold desert night. Their gilded traveling clothes were covered with fine dust.

"Akim! Jelode!" shouted Rahjem. "I think we approach our destination! See the star? It is there above our heads. We must indeed be upon our goal."

"About time, I would venture," said Akim, "My sitting parts are well worn."

"Ah, indeed, I am so pleased to agree," said Jelode."

As the three camel riders drew closer, the woman's baby was being born. Joe jumped up and about, prancing through the straw and scattering braying sheep and goats and pigs in all directions. "Get back, you! Out of the way!" he shouted. The three dogs, of course, rose up, sniffed the air and approached the woman, who was lying down on the floor of the barn. Two began to lick her feet and one started on her face.

Joe was not amused. "Away, all three of you little beasts! Leave her be!" The dogs, admonished, shrank away and cowered back under the hay, only three brown heads with black eyes glittering sticking out to watch and sniff.

The baby was born in due time just before midnight. A boy, he was cleaned by Joe with rough cloth and wrapped in one of Joe's shirts to then be placed in the woman's arms. The three dogs approached and were petted by the woman and allowed to snuffle and lick the new baby. The three travelers arrived on their mounts and jumped down.

Rahjem was stopped by Joe at the entrance to the barn, "Hey, wise guy, what do you want?"

"Actually, dear honored sir, we are *three* wise guys. We have come a long way to see the baby and bring him gifts. We have seen it in the stars and have been guided here. This baby can bring peace to our troubled world. May we enter?"

The three dogs were intrigued. They joined Joe at the entrance to the barn and began to bark and jump and howl while wagging tails so hard one might think they would fly loose from their little bodies. "Um, Okay," said Joe. "The dogs seem to like you."

The men entered, leaving the camels to fend for themselves among the barn animals that had wandered out during the exchange between the men. "Ah," said Akim, "We have gifts for the baby." He peered over at the mother and child and motioned to Jelode. "Place them down, Jelode, there, near the dogs."

Carrying the three satchels from the camels, Jelode produced a small chest. He opened it and it was full of cold coins. He reached again and produced an ornate urn, and then another. All three items were placed on the ground next to the baby and its mother.

"Behold," exclaimed Rahjem, "We bring gold and rare anointments of great treasure. Please accept our gifts on the eve and morning of such a great day!"

"Well, my, thank you," said the woman, babe in arms, "I don't know what to say."

While Joe watched, nonplussed, the dogs knew what to do. They all three descended on the containers. The first pushed its nose into the chest and bit into and swallowed two small gold coins. The other two dumped the urns into the straw and began to roll; eyes wide and feet in the air.

"Ah, no!" shouted Jelode, "For the baby! Not for the dogs! Curse you, all three!"

"Leave my dogs alone, you camel-driven fool!" exclaimed Joe. "I did not invite you here!"

"Please, peace to you all," admonished Rahjem and then held out a hand, palm up. "It is the journey and the future to which we aspire, let the dogs be. Are they not creatures on our earth as well as we?"

The three dogs sure thought so.

They stopped their antics and trotted over to the woman and baby. She said, "Oh, you stink so!" What are we to do?"

The three dogs just sat, shook their heads, ears flapping, and stared up with eyebrows raised. Their biggest concern was dinner but that was handled by Akim who produced hard dried meat for the little dogs and placed it on the straw for them.

Joe had many questions. The woman did as well. The dogs did not; they were full of Akim's dried treats. After a time, Rahjem announced that all should sleep and each person drew a rough blanket over their shoulders and lay down on the straw floor. The woman was given one of the gilded robes to cover herself and the baby. The three dogs each chose one of the travelers with whom to sleep and all was right with the world.

After the spills, the barn smelled really good.

In the morning, Joe would be checking dog droppings for gold.

But that night, three wise guys, three dachshunds and a man and woman and child slept all dreaming of the future of the world.